SILVER SPLITTERS

Tales of the Unsuspected

Gwen Hullah

Published by She and the Cat's Mother

Published by She And The Cat's Mother 2016
SheAndTheCatsMother.co.uk

A CIP catalogue record for this book is available from the British Library.

Paperback ISBN: 9780993552748
Ebook ISBN: 9780993552755

Titles by Gwen Hullah
Safe In Killer Hands: Money, Madness, Murder
Silver Splitters: Tales of the Unsuspected
Safe In Killer Hands: The Original Screenplay

Also
Published by She And The Cat's Mother, in March 2017, Alice Returns Through The Looking-Glass: A Musical Vaudeville Screenplay, (by Zizzi Bonah; script editor Gwen Hullah). Alternative format, Alice Returns Through The Looking-Glass: A Musical Vaudeville Stage Play, (by Zizzi Bonah; script editor Gwen Hullah).

:

CONTENTS

:

Gwen Hullah's collection of compendious stories.

Who are these Silver Splitters, who, like the orchid dares to bloom when its keeper is away on holiday?

Meet the Silver numerals with spear-headed hands who timely seek an alternative in the most unsuspected ways...

SHE KISSED IT WORSE

"A very plain widow with very deliberate ways; who knows the value of medicinal herbs and plants..."

SHE KISSED IT WORSE

Beryl sat picking protruding sultanas from the curved edge of her scone.

Penelope, her longevous friend eyed her covertly, knowing the other's extremes between plain tastes and deliberate ways. She lowered her eyes and drew a discreet comparison. 'Just for one indigestible moment, dear, you reminded me to spray my blighted potatoes with Dithane.'

Beryl was able to smile the comment aside. 'And I'll remind you that someone else's baking is less pleasurable than a defence against poisoning.' Silence fell, but by the look she gave the other woman, it wasn't going to last too long.

Every Thursday afternoon, since retirement, they lighted on each other like lovers always on the verge of a squabble, and yet, somehow they thrived on it. As usual, they were seated at a table within their favourite tea-shop, just a stone throw from the bus station, and for once, Penelope had arrived first and already ordered a cream scone for Beryl, and for herself a portion of apple pie surrounded by a pool of cream. They finished chewing and swallowing in a gradual accumulation of warning signs.

Enviably, Beryl couldn't help but stare, occasionally, at her friend seated opposite her, leisurely stirring not one but two teaspoons of sugar into her cup of tea, which everyone knew would eventually turn to fat, yet made no difference to Penelope's weight whatsoever. Beryl felt a tinge of resentment surface. She had only to look at food to put inches onto her hips, and added to this discern, she could no longer ignore Penelope's sun scorched complexion which reflected as an impressionism from the silver-plated tea-pot to the matching milk jug. Beryl averted her hungry eyes and swallowed the irritation that she could feel building up within her system. Today of all days, she needed her friend's detached advice and agreeable silences – not distractions – she told herself, as she placed the tea-pot abruptly onto a passing waitress's moving trolley – it was obvious Penelope had been lounging idly in her back garden, yesterday, eating strawberries or radishes and sipping iced tea while topping-up her summer tan – just to please herself – no one else to please – Oh, yes, friend Penelope was happily divorced and it showed. It ruddy well showed!

Penelope, conscious of her childhood friend's accentuated staring; strong enough to curdle anyone's cream, she mused. So to break the intensity she leaned forward and at the same time, noting dear Beryl had re-dyed her hair ginger to blot out the silver roots which signalled she was still indulging herself in barefaced speed-dating... still dreaming of love and romance or at the very least, making herself more generally beddable. 'About this speed-dating lark, Beryl?'

'What about it?'

'You must be more careful –'

'Careful –'

'Yes. It's getting out of hand all this harum-scarum of touting for men, numbered from one to twenty; all standing, sitting and each allotted three minutes, wherein, their likes and dislikes are formed instantly and seldom revised, and even worse, my dear, you don't know where they've come from or where they've been...' She was aware what she was saying, and too often, but couldn't help herself. 'And furthermore, you could catch something that you hadn't bargained for.' She paused, seeing she was beginning to ruffle the other's feathers by the familiar habit of her dropping the side-fork onto the plate with a warning clatter. Penelope smiled a little by the sparseness of the response, so decided to stretch her concern. 'You said only last week that the first one barely sat down opposite you before he asserted himself with minimum co-operation by saying, he was too old to be mothered and promptly disappeared to find the nearest public house and –'

'You'll be pleased to know...' Beryl cut through Penelope's concernment abruptly, 'that I've met this man – Lawrence – very well spoken, smells nice and wears well-heeled shoes.' She stopped to catch her breath. 'And over more, I've invited him home for Sunday dinner.'

'What!'

Beryl avoided the other's penetrating eyes by unnecessarily polishing her teaspoon on a serviette before quickly stirring her tea into circular spins. 'He did say quite amiably he would accept my invitation as long as the food wasn't too homely and it wasn't raw –'

'And!'

Beryl showed her palms by way of yielding to some other temptation.

Penelope's eyes opened wider and her mouth went smaller as though she was kicking off pinching shoes. 'Men,' she said tersely, 'especially selfish men, Beryl, do not look at the mantelpiece while they are poking the fire.'

Their meeting ended in spoonerism chaos.

:

The following Thursday found Beryl seated at a far corner table among bamboo and greenery with singleness of attention focused upon the tea-shop entrance. She was not disappointed. Penelope, wearing the flowered, silk dress, the one she had worn to celebrate her dissolution of marriage, sublimely curved a figure eight round her sturdy sun-tanned legs as she moved with quiet dignity, turning her head that way and this way until she caught sight of Beryl shaded by the evergreen, and as she advanced towards her, Beryl leaned across the table to remove her copious handbag from the opposite chair, a custom impossible to break, knowing

Penelope would be late, all too often late, enough to drive anyone else silly. 'I've already ordered Bratwurst hot dogs,' she said pleasantly, settling back onto her chair and folding her hands complacently, which hid pure will.

Penelope could see through this deceptive habit and entered into the game. She sat down in a casual manner while noting dear Beryl had not taken her coat off. She fleetingly wondered if she was feeling under the weather, or had the Sunday meal and dessert proved too much for her? She decided to place her toe in the water first. 'You don't look over clever, my dear. Are you starting with a summer cold?' She paused artfully. 'If nothing else, I can't help but notice you've not bothered to take your coat off.'

Beryl's grey eyes changed colour according to her perfectly natural impatience. 'I've been through a lot lately what with one thing after another, in fact a day seems to stretch into days.' She unfolded her hands and smoothed her disarranged ginger curls.

'Poor old you.' Penelope patted her hand gently. 'You do look tired and drawn, and your coat looks far too heavy for you. And there's no wonder because according to impeccable sources...'

There was a moment of silence which allowed them to weigh each other up.

Beryl was thinking – Penelope should learn not to pay too much attention to rumour because I will not always find her inconsistences appealing...

As for Penelope, she perceived by the look behind the darkened eyes, Beryl was wondering: How much shall I tell her about so many false starts with my speed-dating? It's so unlike me to respond to pressure. Feeling the other's minatory stare she prudently said, 'Truth can be blamed, but never shamed!' She paused as the waitress fetched their order to the table, then left.

Beryl smiled her thanks across the lightly smoked snack. 'On second thought, I'll take my coat off, then you can tell me how your week has favoured you, as I can see you do look quite untarnished.'

'That's because the company I keep these days is unnaturally sparse of unattached men.' Penelope's voice was calm as a mountain lake, 'and quite unlike yours, which I gather, is full to the brim with perfect strangers.'

Beryl fell silent, almost as if she was thinking solely of the continental food she was eating or the raspberry sorbet to follow. She swallowed noisily. Then looked Penelope straight in the eyes. 'Confirmed bachelors and widowers, I find, have acquired all the skills of evasive strategy as soon as they get the faintest waft of a single woman with a spark of romance or love reflecting from her eyes, then they're off like a skunk out of a bolt-hole,' she said this with a flash of undiluted dislike in her lovely grey eyes which Penelope thought was wondrous to behold.

Still marvelling while reaching for the mustard pot, Penelope began to spread a wafer thin layer upon the pork sausage. 'I've been wondering, transiently, of course, when are you going to get round to mentioning your latest speed-date, Lawrence? Did he turn up for Sunday lunch and if so, were you pleasantly surprised or disappointed?'

'I thought you'd never ask!' Beryl's face came alight with possibilities. 'I'm sure you'd take a shine to him if you had to meet. He has a very expressive face, long legs, trim figure which he takes great care of, and a good head of hair – silver – and not a split end in slight –'

'No signs of irritable bowel syndrome,' interrupted the other disparagingly, 'or an increasing struggle against his equilibrium or his sex drive?'

Beryl could see her friend failed to go along with her aspirating regard towards a new relationship. She took a bite out of her sausage. 'At our age, Penelope, a new man in one's life is rather like curry kisses. There's bound to be a spark that can be kindled.'

'I find your observations cringe-making.' Penelope made a face. 'Particularly when we both know what happened to your late husband who always looked after his own extremities and look where that got him!'

'At my age...' The widow brushed the bread crumbs from her sensible cotton dress. 'One can't always remember the finer details –'

'But I can!' Her friend's eyebrows alone indicated this. 'Remember? Autumn crocus sap which your Jon drank, thinking that was mead!' The keepsake fell from unguarded lips to lay before them – again – unburied.

Beryl's eyes darkened. 'The accident was a gift, and its sharp edges have become bevelled over the years.' She took another mouthful from the smoked sausage and continued to speak while chewing. 'Let me tell you something, Penelope. The only way anyone can survive their emotions is simply to feign not to have them. A cop-out, I know, but it works.'

Penelope averted her gaze from such an integrated picture of untarnished guilt. It had crossed her mind more than once that her oldest friend could do herself more good if she enrolled onto an evening decorum course, instead of evening speed-dating venues. She dabbed the grease from her moving lips. 'I know you're not yourself these days, in fact, the more I think about you, the more you worry me, particularly since you subscribed to speed-dating. You're just not the same person you use to be!'

'Tommy-rot! I've never been more like myself, otherwise I would be someone else completely. I'm still punctual, still breathing perfectly soundly, still wiping my bottom clean and I still don't throw out anything that might come in handy, while you, Penelope, can neither mention speed-dating calmly, nor refrain from constantly mentioning it.' Beryl's breasts heaved with indignation. 'You should stop chumming up with so many allotment people who wilfully sabotage their neighbours' competitive vegetables if they grow larger than their own.'

The chide Penelope refused to accept, but she accepted the raspberry sorbet with good grace. 'About this Lawrence business. Did he show up on your doorstep last Sunday?' She looked inquisitively at Beryl, and was glad to see she wasn't tensing when asked, again, about him.

'Yes.' The widow's eyes were bright with pursuit. 'A perfect gentleman by anyone's standards, which is more than I can say about the others.' There was a look of secrecy about her which the other woman recognised and particularly begrudged. This hardy to softly came from something that pleasured her and she was keeping it from her, in fact, she'd seldom seen Beryl so animated, at least not since husband Jon left – left her decidedly better-off.

Penelope shook her head quickly, unsettling the dark memories that had suddenly gathered there. Oh yes, her friend had always been a dark horse, whose abilities were something quite shocking – 'Is he...? He can't be? He's dead, isn't he?' He never bothered to read labels: 'Always greedy.' She'd responded, bursting into tears of accomplishment: 'He's dead!'

Struggling to sound friendly, Penelope persisted. 'Promise me you'll be very careful of these fringe daters with their unfamiliar names and faces. They can and do have repercussions. Remember the retiree from Yaxley whom you invited to your tea-garden party?'

'As if I could forget.' Beryl was suddenly expansive in her gestures. 'He ate all the salmon sandwiches and –'

'Left all the crusts!' encouraged Penelope. She loved gossip.

'Ate all the sponge drops, coconut macaroons and semolina biscuits and –'

'Everything but the pig's grunt.'

Beryl demurred, as the waitress fetched the pot of tea for two which usually they took in turns to pour out. Today, Penelope seized the impromptu moment and poured, not wanting the other to dry-up. She was not disappointed – dear Beryl's tongue was loosening.

'Then he proceeded to drink a whole bottle of Canary –'

'Wharf –'

'Wine! We knew we were on a disaster course, but at our age, sensibility flies out of the window. It's the power and pleasure of fantasies reassuring us that we aren't half-dead but still alive.'

It was a though, thought Penelope, dear Beryl was going to a confession – unburdening her ill-behaviour – asking her friend to bless, and absolve her misdemeanours – which brought her thinking strictly back to Lawrence – the man with the piercing blue eyes and silver-white hair, shod in shiny patent shoes. He must be someone special – and more to the point – life without Beryl's company was unthinkable – the daily telephone calls, Thursday snacks, the country weekends – these would all come to an end if she settled for a new man, and she would be edged out of their longevity friendship; the outlook for herself would be overwhelmingly bleak. Who else would she share gossip with, and laughter, even their squabbles now seemed precious... She blinked away the barbs of resentment. She would have to persuade dear Beryl and if that didn't work – well – then she'd simply have to take a leaf out of the other's book, and...

'After he squeaked the cork back into the empty bottle...' Beryl was saying, 'he said that he hoped his postcoital conversation wasn't incongruous, and that I'd not to let it impinge on beddie-byes.' Encouraged wickedly by her divorcee friend's reaction, the teller thought – She's no idea of the fun she's missing... She'd rather enjoy the minutuae tip-bits of my speed-dating, or rather weed her riotous allotment, or simply gain a tan instead of a new partner. 'Yes. Beddie-byes.' Beryl responded excellently. 'After all, what does a few cuddles and baby names cost?' She drank her tea greedily. 'I don't mind telling you, he actually cursed the whole time he undressed until he collapsed exhausted onto the edge of the bed with his underpants twisted inside his trouser legs which cut of his circulation...'

'How like a man to use the skills of evasive tactics

when...'

'His arms and mine weren't strong enough to re-position him onto the bed as his body sagged – my back caved in – and all we could do was blame each other, then, applying an independent mind, he remembered his blood pressure and his heart pills.' She caught Penelope's disconcerted stare. 'Yes! Yes. I managed to slip one under his tongue, and he rallied round – eventually – he was too dependant, so –'

'I thought you said he was fifty-three?'

'Eighty-three in broad daylight, but I was not perturbed by all this,' she said gallantly. 'After all, it may be that most of us care or love because we need to do so, not because we find someone who does not deserve it.'

'That's as may be.' The divorcee stirred her tea thoughtfully. 'All the same, dear Beryl, it must have been close to a let down.'

Beryl poured herself another cup of tea. 'The occasion...' she replied grandly, 'had its compensation. He gentlemanly gave me £50 in notes, and I cut his toe nails.'

:

Several days passed without the daily telephone call from Beryl, despite Penelope's intermittent phone calls which were not answered, causing her uneasiness and constant worry. Had dear Beryl fallen down the stairs and broke her neck? She rapidly blinked the image away. Or perhaps a reoccurrence of bronchialitus – but it was summer, not winter

– or maybe... the milliner took a pin from her mouth and selected a place in the mohair hat for it, then holding it at arms-length she began to turn her creation round and round in a chasten manner, mentally chastising Beryl for not acknowledging her calls – including the knocking on her front door. Nor answering her elegy recited through the movable flap and brush. Perhaps on reflection – a trifle common, but all the same, not enough to alert the neighbours, and just to let Beryl know of her visit, she'd left a jar of home-made pickle on the doorstep.

:

The following Thursday found Penelope arriving at the cafe on the three o'clock chimes, only to catch no glimpse of dear Beryl. Disappointed, trying not to be conspicuous while conscious of the turning heads of the regulars seated at their usual self-appointed tables. She lengthened her stride and headed for the corner table next to the fruit machine, comforting herself with the thought – if Beryl didn't show up – she could fill the time appearing to be a game-player.

Eventually, a waitress took her order. One toasted teacake and a black coffee – she made both last the next hour, until a regular waitress cleared the table and casually mentioned that she'd served her friend and a distinctive looking gentleman with a crop of silver-grey hair – wearing patent shoes. They had ordered two baskets of sweet and sour pork with wild rice, but no dessert; and by the intimacy – he seemed like an old flame.

'A neighbour!' Penelope blustered, ordering a pot of strong tea to combat the hard water, to be served with a jug of single cream. Indulgence to extreme, she knew, but she needed the nourishment and time to think – moreover, she didn't trust her legs to carry her through the exit doorway due to a quiver of pure jealously rippling up and down her spine. Intimacy! He must have spotted the 'Lowry' painting hung on the parlour wall – the Dresden collection and the family silver displayed ostentatiously on every shelf. How blatant and crass dear Beryl could be – not that she ever called her that even in her own mind – until now. Meanwhile, just to give herself something to do, she poured the cream liberally over the back of the spoon and watched it ooze smoothly to the bottom of the cup, and gradually emerge in rich circles to finally mantle the whole surface; which brought her disquiet thoughts back to dear Beryl and that Lawrence.

Raising the teacup to her moving lips she drank deeply while wondering where did they go to after leaving here? Gliding round the dance floor at the senior tea-dance...? But Beryl had two left feet... Perhaps traipsing round the nearest supermarket looking for buy-three-for-the-price-of-two...? Beryl always liked a bargain... Or maybe climbing Brimham Rocks just for the view with a bunch of strangers? Strangers like the ones she meets, briefly, through the dating agency. And now – dear Beryl, had stopped being splendid.

She poured herself another cup of tea grudgingly admitting that since her happy divorce, she was unfrequented by male company and female married friends except for dear old Beryl, and as for their squabbling, no matter, they usually ironed them out before a Thursday... But not this Thursday. Now – What? Penelope carried on with the conversation in her head. Hats for all seasons! Her exclusive millinery business she had built up from scratch to give herself solace and independence. A lifestyle associated with all those outrageous Ascot hats designed for the ladies of the Curling Cartwheel Club suddenly seemed frivolous compared to a treasured lifelong friendship. For a second she didn't feel too bad, then it all felt too bad. Their friendship had to come first and this Lawrence sounded like a real threat. He would be taking first place, and that would never do.

Penelope raised her elegant hands to her throbbing temples. What was it her solicitor had said to her more than once: 'If a problem, Miss Marsella, is faced head on with sufficient degrees and accuracy then the solution has already been formulated...' The clatter of falling coins from the fruit machine brought her back to the present. Not a willing idler, she drank up, then covered the bill with a note and without a backward glance, left the tea-room.

:

'I will sit tight and wait for Beryl to contact me first,' Penelope was saying to her tabby-cat with brindled streaks, lounging stupendously on its favourite chosen place: a goose feathered bolster. She was sharpening scissors ready for cutting through mohair cloth, the beginnings of an exclusive design, chalked out solely for her winter collection. 'And I don't mind telling you, there they were, as bold as brass, strolling arm in arm through the precinct yesterday afternoon, I mean, who would not recognise Beryl a mile-off – plodding along with her feet pointing at quarter to and quarter past three, and dressed in her serviceable clothes, always bought for lasting rather than show.' She paused to angle herself in alignment with the cutting of a gregarious pattern designed with Mrs Lipmann in mind, the founder of the Women's Curling Cartwheel Club. 'And as for that Lawrence, well, no one would mistake him for Father Christmas with his clean shaven face and silver-white hair, all dragged fiercely back into a ponytail – and no!' She glared at the cat who was licking a paw moist then proceeded to wash its striped face at leisure. 'No, I was not stalking them. I merely happened to be in town to stock up with haberdashery – he was doing all the talking no doubt to keep the ball rolling, because Beryl is always sparing with her words so this dating lark will definitely have its teething problems.' Penelope nodded her head meaningfully at the tabby cat. She felt that she could tell the purring cat anything and its indifference somehow, had a calming effect on her – but not today. 'They didn't see me of course. I draped my chiffon scarf around my head on seeing them enter Jarrods and Simpsons, then saunter towards the fruit and vegetable section – and believe it or not...' The milliner gathered up the cut-outs and quite against her better nature, threw them down onto the work bench, then savagely pinned the shapes into perfect order. 'This Lawrence...' She sounded almost audible to herself and even darling tabby cat's purring seemed to her to carousal in agreement. 'This Lawrence personage selected a peach then placed it beneath his nostrils, to quickly return it onto its purple groove before choosing another and turning it this way and that way before replacing it, only to pick another to another until he finally picked the perfect one and rouged his cheek with it before placing the ripe peach to his open mouth to take a huge bite out of it then replace it!' Her mouth began to water as she relived the occasion. 'And I can tell you, I grabbed hold of the nearest staff member who was stacking the forced rhubarb and pointed him out, while saying that this kind of behaviour was not conducive to human health or profit, and she quickly agreed it wasn't sanitary and marshalled him off towards a door marked: Private. As for myself, I turned on my heel and left the premises feeling somewhat triumphant.'

:

Three weeks went by before Beryl telephoned Penelope, wherein these anxious days, she had designed hats, hats, and more eccentric hats, whether they would sell or not, she neither cared nor bantered over. She was too beset by mortification due to Beryl's lack of communication which had forced her to return, the previous week, to Beryl's home. She'd had no alternative but to climb over the evergreen hedge – to rattle the bolted tea-garden's side-door repeatedly – cooeeing – then reduced to squinting through the cat grille set in the solid door, to spying the pair of them – Beryl sprawled on a cane chair with her frock above her knees showing her winter-white legs, and Lawrence lounging at her feet, his silver hair almost invisible except when the sun caught it – often – and neither indicated they heard – and now, Beryl had decided to phone in the time of her own choosing. She instinctively knew it was her. It was something in the sound of the ringtone, perversely she allowed it to continually ring before lifting the receiver.

'Hello! Hello!' boomed Beryl. 'Is that you, Penelope?'

Penelope served her with a careful silence, wherein she sorted out her feelings, wondering if a time scale should be set for mortification, while at the same time thinking... I must not sound churlish or perturbed by her absence or she'll immediately say I'm jealous of her new-found companion. 'Yes. Yes.' She sounded civil enough to her own ears. 'I still live here above the shop and a good job too. It's been hats, hats and more hats. They are the peppers that spice up my life.' She knew Beryl would know she was overweening, but she said it anyway. 'In fact...' She lifted her voice. 'I think of my clients' happiness rather than my own as a device for getting to sleep.'

'Are you sure, my dear, that you're not just making more work for yourself. You're a retiree, like me, remember...?' She paused as though distracted, but long enough for Penelope to hear a male voice in the background saying:

'Oh aye. A retiree that made such an athletic leap over your hedge and nearly overshot it –'

'With all your charm and good heartedness, dear,' interrupted Beryl sharply, 'that emanates from you, it's so natural, but not everyone has the patience to look inside or to...'

'Shout through a cat-flap until her head wobbled...'

Penelope's eyes widened as she strained to hear more.

'I think I have a crossed line, Penny, dear, I'll see you Thursday.' She rang off.

:

Thursday afternoon found Penelope with one foot over the tea-shop door-sill and the other on the pavement. She was still in two minds as to whether she should be the first to come round after hearing that Lawrence's last words – 'Needs a psychiatrist,' transmitted down the landline, just before Beryl had slammed the phone down.

Penelope swallowed her distaste. Something would have to be done about him – consciously, she rearranged her expression. It would never do to allow herself to look ugly in the public arena or in any reflective window. She needed a plan. A riddance plan if she couldn't talk dear Beryl out of this three-is-a-crowd business. The arrival of this Lawrence had highlighted her own single state which was a different matter. She squared her shoulders and adjusted the outrageous garnished hat on her noble head and stepped inside the room to look expansively around until she caught sight of Beryl, already seated looking unusually lasciviously dressed in a purple taffeta dress with a very low cut sweetheart neckline, and on closer inspection a flared skirt which fluted round her ample sun-singed legs – and on her broad feet, she noted, open-toed shoes which revealed adhesive plasters wrapped around the smaller members of her feet. She felt her eyes moisten. Dear Beryl, must stop harbouring this sadist at once.

'I've already ordered lasagne with all the fillings and trimmings, my dear. Just to set us up till tea-time,' Beryl said incisively, by way of a greeting. She was in two minds as to whether Penelope had heard Lawrence's over-thwart rebuking, furthermore she was well aware that sometimes they prevaricated for the privilege of selecting their bite to eat.

Penelope's painted red lips creased into a rose. 'I don't like to say this, Beryl, but I'm going to say it anyway. I hardly recognise you.' Her eyes raked the other up and down with the diligence of a curry-comb on a cow's hide. 'You look for all the world to see as a floosy woman.' She struggled to sound friendly. 'It's that Lawrence influence, isn't it.' Miss Marsella knew she could sound sibilant. 'He's turning you into a soaker.' She needed to sit down, before she fell down.

Beryl's face came alight with gratification. 'Lawrence spotted it on a mannequin in the Help the Aged charity shop window. He said it would set me off a treat –'

'Charity shop!' Penelope's eyes wandered into vagueness.

Patting the other's hand, Beryl smiled generously. 'It's not outlandish for older women to want a bit of fun. It's far better than passing time on in some strange antiseptic institution, besides, I've so much to tell you...'

And while Beryl talked, laughed and talked about a bus trip to Cumbria, ploughman's lunches, walking bare foot on sandy beaches, hiking on and off bridle paths... Penelope thought – If her belated husband had not drank from the mislabelled bottle of plant juice she would surely have talked him to death...

'That's him – over there –' she'd say, pointing a forefinger while walking over to her sideboard and automatically lifting the hem of her sensible skirt to dust the pot urn placed on a crochet doily. 'I talk to him on and off, when it suits me, of course...' and her large grey eyes she would use to great advantage... Penelope blinked herself back to her murderess friend, hearing her boldly saying:

'And you're the most aggressive listener I've ever known. Not like Lawrence. He's like a tomcat stalking on hot slates...' She leaned forward. 'From one to another and the gatepost, I sense a snaffle is between his frustration against the inadequacy of life and the fear of dying...' She chose a utensil and began to eat, still talking. 'I know it's intriguing and difficult to picture what with your good health, safe bank account and faultless yet eccentric ways.'

Penelope demurred. 'Friendship, like marriage, I always think is an accumulation of warning signs and nobody knows that better than you or I.' She smiled her professional smile. 'I've not let the grass grow under my feet while you've both been trailblazing. I've arranged an exclusive showcase in my millinery room displaying my new range of fabulous hats which includes next season's exclusive creations. There are several ennobled descents invited plus more than two others that you've met. Mrs Lipmann of the Curling Cartwheel Club, Rick Thingamajig, the Town Cryer and of course the Mayor and Mayoress of Grassington, and most importantly, dear Beryl, I'd love to meet Lawrence, so I'm inviting you both as my special friends...' Penelope's eyes sparkled with purpose as they met and held the brilliant grey eyed stare while reaching out to touch the other's plump hand holding a forkful of Latinity food. 'There will be a delectation of cheeses, biscuits and your favourite wine... Pichon Longueville.'

After a slightly longer delayed reply than she'd intended, Beryl, knowing only too well how her friend's charismatic power of persuasion and the assurance of being entertained by seeing all those extraordinary hats, and meeting her fantastical clientele with the exchange of the latest gossip, which Penelope also served up as a delicious dessert on every Thursday's tete-a-tete, even the squabbles now seemed priceless. 'Yes. We'd love to come and thank you for your invitation... but on one condition, Lawrence is rather partial to '61 Palmer.'

Penelope nodded perhaps a trifle fast. 'I've already replenished my wine stock for the occasion which funnily enough includes your request and he does sound like a gourmet. I hope he doesn't smoke or it will ruin his palate. It would then taste like turpentine.'

A little smile touched the corners of Beryl's lips. 'I'm sure you'll take a liking to him. His bark is worse than his bite.' She lowered her gaze, thinking – I'm not certain if she'd overheard his choice of words, maybe she didn't take in what Lawrence said because her stripe of jealously always makes her deaf to anything she doesn't want to hear...

Pin-sharp Penelope had read Beryl's thoughts through her eyes – She thinks I'm tone-deaf to any criticism or uncouth language, but she's wrong, even if she gets the mood right. She lowered her eyes to her plate. At this pace he would soon be taking her place and the loss would be too painful to bear, but in the meanwhile, she reminded herself – I must not oppose the relationship... concentrate. Plan. Expiry date.

:

The Marsella Montpelier showcase was a triumphant affair in more ways than one. Her exclusive brand of hats were all modelled with panache by the ladies from the allotment, who wore little black dresses with accessories; white gloves to hide calloused hands and finger nails indicating the gardeners' insignia. After much ooh-la-la, the purse-proud guests purchased their selected choices, then skilfully directed to the hospitality area, held in the hostess's back garden; wherein, last week the ladies had restrained the meandering roses and wild honeysuckle to the periphery walls, and dead-headed the border flowers who now lifted their floral heads above the smooth, striped lawn.

Naturally, Penelope sublimely re-greeted her clientele on Christian name terms, with Beryl at her elbow portraying a look of come-and-get-it on her homely face as she gripped a tray with both hands, on which glasses had been placed, all filled with sparkling champagne.

Mrs Lipmann helped herself to a glass of champagne. 'There's nothing quite like having a daily who obliges with little to no exercise.' She looked Beryl up and down as

30

though she was a scullery maid, hesitated, then decided to stretch a point. 'The dress that you're wearing, I seem to recognise it...' She moved her eyes to take in Lawrence, almost without affectation, who was leaning against the laburnum tree with the sunshine casting rays of light through its branches to highlight his silver hair. He was holding, she noted sagaciously, a bottle of '61 Palmer in one hand, and a glass in the other which he now tilted to his mouth. 'Yes...' She returned her gaze to Beryl's bold stare, and was prepared to give her more of her attention. 'Yes.' She took another sip of champagne and swallowed it attentively. 'Yes, and I also recognise the man who came with you earlier –'

'Lawrence –'

'Lawrence did you say? I'm sure I heard him say Maurice.' She closed her eyes and furrowed her brow. 'Let me think. I never forget a face.' She opened her eyes as quickly as she'd closed them. 'Yes. He was taking up space while I was browsing in Rawlinson's Auction Rooms, last week. He came in carrying a Lowry painting and seeking advice –'

'Did you say... a Lowry picture?'

'Indeed. It was signed and dated. An original – apparently.'

Beryl's large grey eyes widened and her mouth went tighter, while her rosy complexion slowly inflamed, spreading down her ample neck to her heaving breasts as she re-gripped the tray handles. 'Did you see the title?'

'More or less. Something pertaining to industrial surroundings, and I rather took a liking to it myself.' Mrs Lipmann smiled, a studied, expert smile. 'This champagne is delicious. Mind if I have seconds?' She reached out to place the empty glass back onto the tray, while taking a second helping without batting an eyelid. 'Jewellery. Priceless jewellery scattered in a chocolate box. Yes. I heard him saying quite plainly that his wife had passed on, so he needed the money to give her a grand send off... and furthermore –'

'Which day of the week was this?' Beryl's tone of voice carried obscure implications which was not lost upon the other woman's inspiration, aware via idle talk, that this very plain widow with very plain ways knew the value of medicinal herbs and plants. Encouraged by the widow's reaction, the informer carried on talking indiscreetly.

'Last Thursday. Now that, I do remember well because I saw you in The Kettle and Pot with Penelope, and you was wearing this second-hand dress and she was wearing one of her calmer creations.' Mrs Lipmann paused resolutely. 'Yes. That's him. It's the pig-tail that gives him away.' She patted Beryl's arm with terrible pleasure. 'You should wear flat shoes, my dear, they're much kinder to the facial expressions, but enough gossip for now. I'd better hurry along to the marquee before all the crustless sandwiches are eaten.' And off she went.

Beryl, left to her own device, lifted the tray shoulder high then dropped it straight down onto the flagged patio with a crash and tinkling of broken glass. Penelope, alerted, glanced over her shoulder and thought for a moment that dear Beryl had tripped over her tabby cat... but no. She was standing perfectly ridged, arms hung by her sides, fists clenched and her mouth wide open. Alarmed, Penelope hurried to her side and peered into her friend's distorted face, plainly seeing pin-heads of perspiration settling on her pallid forehead. 'Oh, crikey! Beryl! You're not suffering heatstroke or a heart attack? Not today, of all days.'

Beryl ogled back at her. 'Just help me to get some private space. I need... a large brandy to get me off the ground. Then – I'll need your advice and careful silences.'

:

'I knew it! I bloody well knew something like this would come from that dating lark. A lesser woman or a saner one would have been thrown off guard, but you, dear Beryl, are neither less nor sane, and for what it's worth, there's one consolation, these investments of yours have been returned and put back in their places, for now. No wonder he's booked you both into a package holiday next month so he can buckle back for the auction date... or...?' Their eyes met and held in tempered suspicion. 'Would he... could he... be planning your demise?'

:

33

'That's settled,' said Beryl boldly, hearing Lawrence's stilted footsteps approaching before he rounded the millinery room doorway, holding the empty wine bottle by the neck.

'Who's settled what?' His eyes fastened onto the two women sat indulging themselves with a fresh brew of tea. They turned their faces towards him, seeing a resentful man, jealous of women whose abilities and earning power he'd never been able to equal, and he'd kept it a secret – until now.

'Come and join us for a refreshing cup of tea,' said Penelope pleasantly. 'On the other hand, if you feel so inclined, I've a spare bottle of '61 Palmer in my wine cellar which I'd love to give you both towards celebrating your holiday on the Isle of Man –'

'I'm not sure to what extent such patronising is sincere,' he interrupted bluntly. 'To my mind, you're not quite... quite, but... very nearly...' He rolled the words round on his tongue as though they had flavour.

Their wearing smiles appeared congenial. They had no intention of him even to guess.

'What's settled?' he repeated, not returning their smiles. Instead be began to strut around the room touching equipment, and feeling materials in a monitory way.

Not letting their guard drop, Beryl spoke amiably. 'We'd love to accept your generous offer, wouldn't we Lawrence?' Her manner was so pleasant that it was hard for even Penelope to believe dear Beryl and herself was not purposely going to inflict a nasty surprise on this perfidious man.

Pitching her voice low enough for Lawrence to be able to pretend not to hear. Penelope said, 'I've been bursting to tell you, Beryl, I've had a substantial offer from Bolderson and Blotts to clear the racks of all the vintage wines. They said there is an enviable labelled collection there and I'm tempted –'

'I'm not surprised.' Beryl sounded lugubrious. 'Your ex-husband was such a connoisseur and you can't take it with you once you've gone. It's high time you cleared the cellar out, it's such an encumbrance what with you being a diabetic.' The lying, she told herself, was only temporary and women were so resourceful when betrayed. She rubbed her friend's hand in an absurd manner, which at any other time would have been highly irritating to the other's senses.

But today, Penelope knew there would be no turning back. They were setting a trap. A trap that had to work. 'I really would like you to accept the one remaining '61 Palmer, a small gift I know, but nevertheless, given with my blessing.'

'These random words are like a bad discussion in a loony-bin.' He felt threatened by the solidarity of their long friendship and opulence. He had to put a spoke between their wheels of companionship, and he'd every intention of carrying out the disposal of the acquired-by-habit widow and fleecing her of her wealth. She wouldn't be the first nor the last, but foremost, he knew he'd have to settle the friend's ash first. She was the tricky one. Stealthily he hugged his secret close to his being whilst the condescending bottle of wine still cruised through his system... Blame the fermented juice, he told himself, and when sober, pretend to have no recollection on what had gone before.

Turning away his premeditated thoughts he maliciously decided to rock the boat by dispensing with civility, having already determined to use desultory language in great copious colour with pervert ideas – which suggested a surprising assortment of themes on senior citizenship, and all the wear and tear of weaknesses.

Penelope blinked the affront aside with all the finesse she could muster, then turned cow-eyed to Beryl, saying cautiously, 'He talks to women as though we are men.'

Beryl, out-spoken Beryl, could not trust herself to reply. Instead she opened her handbag and took out a powder compact and powered her bulbous nose thoroughly – thinking... Why had I hoped, even dreamed, that this man could enhance my life – help me to fill the next twenty or thirty numbered years? She felt herself squirm with humiliation, listening to his vulgarity while trying to remember what if anything she really knew about him...

Sensing the changed atmosphere within the room, he

became adamant. Tetchily so, saying, 'And where's the bloody gents. I need a slash!'

Rising quickly to her feet, trying to keep the anger out of her voice, Penelope said, 'Down the passage as far as the junction, then turn left. It's the door next to the store room.' She crossed the room purposely to open her work-room door.

Urgently he followed behind her. Close enough for her to hear him enunciate, 'I hope to hell we don't bump into any ugly customers of yours still wearing those fuckin' gaah...gar...loyd hats!'

'He means gargoyle hats,' corrected Beryl, catching them up.

'Gargoyle!' The millinery proprietor spun round and stared at him like a mare out of season. 'Gargoyle hats!' She tried to find words to match her repellence. It was impossible.

'If I have to stand here much longer, I'll piss myself.' Lawrence began to unbutton his trouser fly-opening.

Distraction seems to offer the middle road, thought Beryl, pushing passed them. 'Come along, Lawrence. I'll show you where the toilet is situated. We don't want you to stain the carpets.'

Head down, he muttered something they didn't need to know.

Then it happened. Just as they arrived at the junction of the passage way, Mrs Lipmann suddenly rounded the far corner still wearing her newly bought outrageous hat and carrying a doggie bag. She halted, then waving her arms wildly, she pointed her forefingers at Lawrence, shouting, 'That's him! I knew it would come to me eventually. Stop him ladies! Stop him. He's –'

'Another bloody gaarr...goole,' he bawled out drunkenly, staggering to the left and grabbing at the nearest door knob to wrench the door open, to waver dangerously on the threshold – only to pitch forward through the opening – seeing too late a flight of stone steps – knowing there was no possibility of turning back – barely giving himself the time to cry out, or to feel the veneer of his life – stripped – before the closure of the killing game.

:

The following Thursday afternoon, found Beryl seated at her chosen table within the tea-room, in a state of ever presence. Her fine grey eyes set off the startling freshness of her complexion, which immediately caught Penelope's attention as she hurried, on time, to meet her with a where-have-you-been look creasing her face.

'Health farm, in the Cotswolds, and what a clarifying experience.' Beryl answered the unspoken question before it could be asked, 'And believe it or not, my dear, I've practically lost a stone in weight. I can tightened my belt by a notch.' She smiled with her eyes – thinking... Dare I tell her I've met a dare-devil stockbroker of reputed character – years

38

younger than me – and we just clicked... but would she approve? She doubted that. Better to wait until the Lawrence business has blown over. She leaned forward. 'I've already ordered toasted teacakes and a pot of tea to tide us over.'

Penelope lowered herself down onto the opposite chair while she absorbed the information, then she said, 'Mrs Lipmann called briefly at the shop this Monday to say that she and her husband had done what they could for that man, in the excellent way of the Methodist faith.' She paused, while the waitress came and went. 'She also said, quite nastily, that she'd never liked you one little bit, and she especially blamed you for befriending an accused criminal undergoing penal servitude, and that you're sins would come home to rouse.'

Beryl's smile remained benignly in place. 'What's all that suppose to mean?'

'I didn't have the courage to ask.' Penelope began to butter her toasted teacake. 'After all, unknowingly, she did the job for us.' She modulated her voice. 'An interested lady from the allotment told me, confidentially, that she'd seen a white, unnamed removal vehicle parked outside Mrs Lipmann's home – a rented house – and she had noticed the flitter was carrying a potted fuchsia magellanica which she could not help noticing was affected by rust.' Penelope began to chew thoughtfully, which accentuated her love of gossip. 'So, my dear, they can't have buried him there – on the other hand...' Her spirits plummeted cruelly as she reached to clutch her friend's hand which was already pouring out tea from the teapot. 'You don't think...' Penelope's voice, solemn and minatory confirmed the impulse to say, 'Would they...? Could they have...? After all my dear Beryl, you've been away from your home for days.'

KEEN TO SHOEHORN

"When a wife's ultimatum leads to a husband's ultimate trap..."

:

KEEN TO SHOEHORN

(Monologue)

:

Gerald, fifty-something. Redundant. His wife has left him until he sorts himself out. He's sat in the conservatory sipping a glass of whisky, looking morose.

Redundant! Anyone would think that a skilled engineer with twenty-six years experience under my belt would be snapped up immediately – but no! And to crown it all, my wife of as many years has left me to go and live with her sister in Malta – conditional – so now I fill the void with a sense of ill-usage. I've been roped in as a joiner-come-handyman to the Local Amateur Dramatic Society. 'The Lads' I've called it if anybody cares to ask. They don't. So, I'm reduced to pottering, tinkering and hammering – taking things apart and putting them 'differently' together again. The producer, Fionia, calls my repairs and designs dismal, which greatly modifies my personality. The end results may be, or not be, aesthetically pleasing to her eye, but after the technical cessation of hostilities, I remind her, by swearing blindly, with my experience of many, many years as a renowned engineer – my last contract being the celebrated Nathen suspension bridge spanning the River Yonder; therefore with my expertise things will work beautifully before the opening of the play – 'The Libertine Poet-Laureate'. A comedy. Rehearsals begins early November.

Pause.

The other evening during designing the 'old into new' backdrops, I heard Fionia's authoritative footsteps resounding on the warped boards. She's a very forthwith woman of a dangerous age with a very determined look in her brown eyes. She's also the sort of female who will do semi-private physical movements a normal lady would not do before a perfect stranger; and my sensibility to recapture that exquisite moment more exact is disappointing – which brings my mind strictly back to my wife, Evelyne.

Pause. Gerald pours himself a cup of coffee from a percolator while holding a letter with an attached postcard in the other hand. He's looking sombrous.

I've just received this letter with a postcard attached all the way from my wife's sister, Adele. She writes to me like an accomplice; disclosing, Evelyne is now determined to find for herself an obliging man who will appreciate her troubadour spirit and who will be willing to accompany her to bridge and dinner parties, which are surprisingly numerous.

Gerald takes a spoonful of sugar and stirs it into his coffee.

Then she goes on to write – between you and me, Gerald, I can see boredom beginning to set in. The social scene in which she has brought herself into is scarce of widowers and bachelors – confirmed bachelors, who are very adroit at evading the hungry huntress with tactics of long-lived practice.

Gerald sips his coffee.

So, Evelyne has taken a fabulous French vocation, paid from her bridge winnings – in Cap-de-Antibes, where she's now acquainted with a flamboyant Count from the valleys who speaks standard English – I speak perfect English, and look where that's got me. Evelyne and I are no longer on speaking terms. Not since my tempered – 'You don't understand the shock of sudden redundancy.' – 'I can understand anything you can,' she shouted back. She was upstairs in the spare bedroom, packing a case, 'and it does no good swearing. Just sort yourself out.' We went to chapel and ate roast beef afterwards. Next morning, she left home.

Gerald starts to loosen his tie then run a finger along the ridge of his collar.

My wife, Evelyne, left a scant letter informing me that our marriage had become dull, suburban and middle-aged. So, she had arranged to stay with Adele in Malta – to reach out to life before the change of life, and before she loses her sanity. As for myself – I had to sit down otherwise I would have dropped down. I felt my heart pounding with alarming speed and my breathing was difficult – but I held on – and reached out to pour myself a noble sized whisky which made me feel better – then worse – and now to top it all, sister-in-law capriciously attached a postcard – a Folies-Bergers postcard that has stretched my skilled imagination to the point that I may not be able to get back to normal.

Go to black.

Gerald, stacking planks of wood in the conservatory. He seems like a different man.

When I come to think about my present circumstances – really think about them, I'm beginning to surprise myself by realising this 'temporal' work – jobbing work at the theatre is proving to be very therapeutic, and for the first time in many, many years I feel relaxed and venerate. In fact, the more I think about myself, I've discovered the freedom to like or dislike anyone, however congenial or uncongenial, who has or has not got talent to act in an amateur or professional manner; and as for the great appetite of the stage-ham who up-stages the entire cast, I have designed a chasten trap-door in the stage floor which I can open – prompted almost entirely by my goodwill – beneath the unexpected orator, and when closed it is perfectly flush with the boards.

Pause. Gerald drinks deeply from his cup as though to savour the brutality.

Yes, I can almost feel a leakage of happiness. I no longer indulge in the absence of intimacy. Yesterday evening Fionia said – or I think she said – after her surprise drop as we wrestled below amongst the newly painted backdrops – 'You, Gerald Paddside, you're rather like an orchid that blooms when its nursery-wife is away on holiday.' Later, much later, it did cross my mind, Evelyne would have put the damper across by saying – rudely: 'the Sunday papers would have headlined the occasion, Gerald as – getting a superfluous leg over the brush!'

Go to black.

Gerald, sat at his computer in the conservatory.

I'm surfing the internet for engineering vacancies to no avail. It's now three weeks since the theatre closed for the season.

The play: 'The Libertine Poet-Laureate', proved to be a triumph. Four months – all full houses, and to round things off after the final curtain call, the players rallied together for a farewell party. All flowers, drinks, Chinese takeaways and lingering kisses which lasted well into the small hours – as for myself, my true instinct has always been to work behind social framework, so I left Fionia making a song and dance about it as they said their prolonged, 'see you all next season' as though it wasn't soon enough, accompanied by a chorus of bye-byes. Fionia has boundless energy. That's what attracted her to me. 'I'll see you later,' I said, as I watched until the crowd pressed around her and blotted her from sight as they headed for the exit door. I remember feeling convivial as I did the last round of checking no one would be locked in the building, while at the same time switching everything off – when by chance my eye caught the closing of the trapdoor, just a fraction before it levelled beautifully with the floor boards. Curiosity aroused, I went down to the prop-room to investigate and there I witnessed Fionia stark naked – arms and legs flaying amongst the debris of backstage remnants, and the 'local-ham' looking like a falling podium with its perpendicular upright. Startled as a shocked spectator, words failed me – yet – did I hear her garble – 'blooming orchid' or was it my imagination? Dispirited, I retreated through the fire exit door. Only the wearer knows of the shoes pinch.

Go to black.

Gerald, stood in the annex at his work bench draughting new designs. The Teasmade alarm rings. He takes the mashed tea and settles down onto an easy chair.

It's exasperating for a staunchly, rigorous engineer like me to be furnished with commissions from resting amateur actors and kennel-maids, who have seen or heard of my skilled designs and workmanship at the theatre – particularly the stage 'trapdoor' mechanics – consequently I'm inundated for my services – not the 'Fionia kind' – which shattered my fiduciary in women – older women who are sexual – attractive – who want to reach out to life – then blatantly blow chances away. So now my workmanship is strictly business. The ladies who seek my original designs, commonly call them 'cat and dog' flaps – I call them 'domestic quadrupes'.

Gerald leaves his armchair and goes over to a set of drawers, takes out a bottle of whisky and a glass, pours himself a stiff drink. Returns to the chair.

This is my quality time. Through necessity, the business has grown so I've turned the annex into my workshop, and very satisfactory it's turned out to be. Evelyne had it ear-marked for her mother – as an alternative to putting her into an Autumn Time Home, but mercifully the old dear decided to follow the sun and went to live with her daughter – my sister-in-law, across the water.

Gerald takes a sip of whisky, then takes a letter from his pocket. Reads briefly.

It's wholly unpleasant and painful to read that in reality, Evelyne is still 'femme fatale-ing' her way around France despite many, many imponderables – and it's now time, they feel, as a desperate mother and sister; for me to start 'wooing' and reclaiming 'your' wife back into her own home because she's cramping their lifestyle – after all, 'Evelyne must surely be considering how you, her husband, can rescue the marriage,' – they underline – 'Gerald, you just have to show forgiveness and willingness, refuse to have an expiry date alongside your sacred vows, and you must put a stop to Evelyne going in and out of old chapels. They were only built so people could argue about God!'

Go to black.

Gerald arrives home late. He turns the car engine off, but remains seated.

I'm sure I turned the lights off in the annex.

He places a hand to his temple then let's it drop onto the steering wheel.

It's probably optical illusion from the after-effects of the tetanus injection administered by the local doctor earlier. I was bitten by a very heavy dog, with a very savage bite. The house-pet – a Mastiff – became wedged in my 'domestic quadrupe' and refused to be tempted by chunks of raw steak to enable itself to wriggle free. I suppose I should have made allowances for its behaviour, but I didn't want to remove my exacting fixture. With hindsight, perhaps scratching its back or its stomach may have helped it to writher free – instead – on an impulse I twisted its tail – repeatedly – possibly childish, but the motion fitted to my present narrow occupation and the truth of Fionia's monkey love – swinging from one man-branch to another – until I suddenly became aware of shouting and snarling; to the lady dog owner coming between myself and the antagonised Mastiff. She was holding a yard brush aloft and before I could straighten my back, she landed two violent blows upon my head which made me bluster madly and excited the provoked animal to escape snarling. I had a glimpse of razor incisors just before they sank deeply into my arm. I retaliated by aiming a solid thump squarely upon its nose. Instantly, it let out a startled yelp which enabled a painful release. She scolded the dog against the temptation of enjoying a bite – I lengthened my stride. I'm not an anarchist or a fanatic, but I will charge an extra forty per cent onto her account.

Go to black.

Gerald, sat quietly on his own in the bar-room of his local pub. There's a full pint of beer on the table, a hand-reach away.

It's raining outside. I'm feeling chilled; and I've a wet Poodle beneath my chair. I never wanted a dog. Evelyne did, especially after our two children left home to follow their careers.

He lifts his full glass of beer and wets his lips.

I informed them last month that their mother and I were getting divorced. They came home immediately. Moved back into the house. Both paraphrased – that after twenty-six years of married life we could not throw in the towel. They'd feel like orphans! Our son soon found his mother. Where? I didn't ask. He didn't offer. He's an IT man. 'My mother, your wife,' he said – 'confessed the gap year has now lost its spice for her and she's ready to roll up her sleeves and somehow mend the marriage, but you, Dad have to meet her halfway.'

Gerald lifts the glass to his mouth, then puts it down onto the bar table.

My daughter, a window dresser at Larks and Fencers, said from what she's gathered, men emotionally shutdown or find themselves another woman when the wife walks out, or... She stared at me with glittering eyes – she's beginning to look like her mother. 'Did you or did you not, Daddy, during Mummy's absence – necessitate in any degree – think of getting rid of your wife, my mother – Daddy?' I had considered – every now and then – but I denied it with indignation and force. There had been too many reasons to be angry and how long can you stay angry. When Evelyne went away – indefinitely – the heart of our marriage was broken. It was as if the house had been cleaned. So, later I surprised myself how quickly I recovered from Fionia's ill-behaviour, which on reflection suggested it was sadly a somewhat casual, informal affair – which brings my thoughts back again to Evelyne – who use to say, repeatedly – she was determined to stop being miserable and lonely with her husband working long contracts all over the country; then suddenly to find me under her feet all the days' long while harbouring many, so many bitter resentments; wherein – she had decided that sensual women have the same desires as men. Yes, and furthermore, she would like to meet a man of passions and moods – apt to fly into jealous humours which neither would need to take seriously – Well, no! What grown-up man would indulge in humour to excess for the sake of a crazy woman of a certain age – he'd have to sleep with one eye open. I was dismayed to perceive a streak of sadism in her make-up. As for children, if you're not on your guard, they would take over and become the parents, reducing the parents to being the children, and when I became angry with their interfering – they chorused – 'anger is a good sign, Daddy. It shows that the marriage is still alive.' And off both went happily to reclaim their old bedrooms – conditional – commuting daily from home to work, leaving the Poodle with us. This breed doesn't moult. I'm told.

He takes another sip from his glass, then leans back on the chair, arms folded.

So here I am. A regular. Sat in the Blue Boar Inn with a damp dog beneath my chair; drinking a pint of cold beer which I don't even like. I make it last for an hour to justify the one mile walk, here and back. To soften the edges, I call it my 'quiet thinking time', wherein I talk to myself, saying, Evelyne and myself have learnt a huge amount about ourselves and we're working through how to recapture all the good memories and relive them.

Gerald reaches for his glass and takes a drink, then wipes his mouth with the back of his hand.

My wife has settled herself down in the guest bedroom – I've paused, anticipating – occasionally – at the slightly open door, but the vague outline amongst the bedclothes doesn't move or speak. I have the need to sabotage her sobriety in order to break the dead-lock. I've already designed a second contraption. I call it 'Lady-trap' and the exciting part being Evelyne has walked over it. Never tripped over it. It's beautifully flush with the guest room's floor boards. I'm biding my time. One of these days – healing days – when the children are out on a work day.

Fade to darkness.

HOME FRONT

"The mystery of an obscure Peer's disappearance during World War Two. Had he chosen to go away and not come back? Did someone or some others do the choosing for him?"

HOME FRONT

To look at me, no one would ever guess that I'm the daughter of an obscure Lord and the beautiful socialite Lady Claudette Wrothwaite. I'm square, plain and wear cast-off clothes; almost unemployable; and nearly all my exiguous allowance is spent on keeping a roof over my head, as circumstances are considerably reduced since what they were before the Second World War. These days I solely dine on polony and knackwurst sandwiches.

As far back as I can remember, I've always been a fat girl. Nanny use to reinforce this belief as though it was her signature to me being well cared for. Instead of over-feeding; force-feeding, to stop the crying and cantankerous tantrums – a substitute to replace the inattention from Mother and Father, who for one purpose alone, wanted a son. An heir. Instead, along came an unwanted daughter. Me!

This abandonment to me was as conspicuous as a red poppy in a cornfield. At the age of six years, I could no longer restrain myself from asking Nanny: 'Where has Mummy gone?'

For a fleeting moment Nanny stopped combing plumbago through my ginger hair – then she rebuked me sharply. 'I'll not tell you again, Isabella, so listen carefully. Two years after you was born, Mummy came down with tuberculosis and was sent to the mountains to a sanatorium…' She paused to push back a hair grip into my blackened hair, 'and if her Ladyship had adhered to the recommended diet of calves' foot jelly, and extracted blood from the hand-squeezed raw meat, she'd be alive today.' Nanny, a real tartar, had boxed my ears soundly then sent me to my room to cry it out, or come to my senses.

As for Father, Lord James Alfred Philip David Wrothwaite, who had time between running the family estate and representing a safe parliamentary constituency before and during the Second World War, well, he'd disappeared completely from sight – lost in the silence of statistics. I often wondered bitterly had he chosen to go and not come back, or did someone or some others do the choosing for him? After years of relying heavily on my imagination and unrealistic expectations, I ventured to ask Nanny while she had her sanity and before she went voluntarily into a home for the Evening Tides.

Nanny said caustically between convulsive coughing (she'd smoked far too many Woodbines). 'Some people within the body of his voters had hinted at skulduggery, others insinuated default within the black-market system and more than two implied – murder!'

I can't keep forever anticipating, using the same handrail to go down into the past – that's why I volunteered to help within the Redemption Bureau. Their priority being to assist people desperate to find family members who go missing – missing scours the soul raw.

I've learned to drop my plummy accent as some people are not particularly grateful characters. They treat me with familiarity instead of respect, addressing me by any idiom other than Lady, with the manners which would not be tolerated by land-girls or household and requisite sales personnel, so with these chastising thoughts in my mind, I randomly boarded a number 23 bus – my lucky number, chancing a happening to impinge on my thin life. So with nonchalance I settled myself down next to a dark handsome stranger, who I sagely noted, was reading the Thimes.

Casting a sideways glance, I could see the passenger was scanning the obituary columns, so mercifully I closed my eyes against the dearly departed until alerted by the rustling of turning pages, and just in time to pinpoint within the readers' letter page a heading which leapt out at me like a Mother's hand grabbing a runaway child – WW2 Evacuees Reunion to be held at... the rest of the printed words were distorted by the fold in the newspaper. Leaning over, I tilted my head graciously close to the traveller's thigh to perceive the town's whereabouts – Ba...at...pe, suddenly a word clicked into my head – could it be...?

Sensing my proximity, the stranger abruptly gathered the pages together and quickly rolled them into a hollow cylinder, and for one erotic moment I thought he was going to swat me.

'Sorry,' I said, releasing a smile. 'I was resting in delicious isolation.'

His eyes, I noted, were bold and blue which matched his broad dialect when he spoke his impudent expletive.

To break the oncoming flow of exacting reality which I perceived was on the edge of his tongue, I gave a Nanny frown. 'Thank you,' I said, 'for being so frank with me, and with someone you've only just met.'

'Damn right!' the two words were said through a quickly diminished smile as he folded his arms across his chest then to half-close his eyes on me.

Sensing a simulated reverie by way of an escape from further conversing in moments chosen by me, I decided to come straight to the point. 'Call it professional curiosity, but I couldn't help noticing that printed within the readers' letter page an invitation to a reunion of WW2 evacuees, and…'

'Curiosity killed the cat!' He curled the corner of his lip in a manner, no doubt, to deter the faint hearted or the gossipry woman.

I didn't bat an eyelid. I'm aware that over-shared sayings can be used like weapons when mastered, besides, I take perverse pleasure from interviewing any uncongenial individual and make plain my feelings without expressing them. It's the only pleasure I get these days, so I opened wide my arresting green eyes, my best feature – Nanny use to say, often – and rather wildly said, 'That old saying coming from you so glibly sounded extremely fixed as to be heartless. I was evacuated on the first of September, 1939, to Nidderdale…' Mentally I crossed myself – the lie tasted but a moment – 'a depraved child bewildered by feeling abandoned by my parents.' I shuddered going over in my mind what I had just said – the truth – put differently.

His eyes, when I looked into them had a disturbing quality. Blank. When he eventually spoke again his voice was devoid of emotion. 'Twenty-five years ago, this September, a six year old stood unaccompanied with urine trickling down his legs and into his shoes, silently crying amongst hundreds of likewise traumatised children too young to understand why this sudden separation from their mothers and the dispersal to rural areas.' He clenched his jaw, plainly furious with himself for that personal disclosure.

It's the little giveaways that mean a lot. They do count, especially to someone wearing the other shoe.

:

Scanning as usual the events, and lost and found columns within the library reading room, I was excited to find what I was looking for. The Evacuees' Reunion to be held in Banathorpe, the market town that Father had represented. The celebration to be held in the Secondary Modern School, this Friday, three o'clock. Opened by the (retired) Headmistress, Mrs Ulaye. Refreshments: Authentic Bake. A re-echo of WW2. Austerity Fare. All welcome.

Because my interest is so strong, I decided to set off a day early for the reunion, hoping to meet someone who had known or at least remembered my father, Lord Wrothwaite. Armed with an ordnance map I braved the unfamiliar roads with high hawthorn hedges and stone walls screening scenic views, but I had no time for the luxury of observations as such. I'd already been misguided by several misleading signposts pointing their arms in the wrong directions and not being local, I found this practice irksome when I was misguided to a cul-de-sac whereby a dutch-barn with its water trough overflowing housed a gathering of Alpacas, and two hours later, again misguided to a sharp-to-the-smell silo plant which traversed its odour across the countryside like a farm yard midden.

Bearing up, I'm good at that, I've learned not to indulge in the opulence of moods. Too debilitating. So I deliberately drove in the opposite direction. Three hours later, I sighted a stone dwelling with a farm-gate swinging from two chains secured to an oak tree branch. Wiping a clearing on the car window screen, I read the words: Gantlope Inn. The relief was overwhelming. I could have wept at the thought of just seeing one human being, never mind others – but I held on. Resourcefulness doesn't leave a woman just because she's lost.

A pleasant warmth greeted me as I entered the bar room.

The warmness I experienced came from a black-leaded fire range adorned with horse-harness, and long brass fire-irons, crossed, lay before the cast-iron fender whilst burning in the grate two beech logs sparked brightly, filling the boozy air with their resinous fragrance.

The intoxication almost got the better of me as I made my way towards the bar, seeing a handful of men, still wearing their flat caps above rustic faces, sleeves rolled up, knee impression trousers, ankle length, showing long-legged boots. They were sat at leisure, intermittently drinking their pints of beer while playing dominoes, and I couldn't help hearing the clicking of the bone spotted lozenge shapes abruptly cease as they became aware of a woman in a man's domain. My intrusion was an emergency, and already the day seemed too long. Moving sharply, but with nobleness, I headed for the bar attendant, whose appearance was construed by the shadows of draped bunting and the shade of a large placard whereon written in bold letters, the wartime slogan: Home Front.

Feeling that I was getting warmer to my predetermined intention, I tried not to look like a stray bonhomie who had nowhere else to go because I'd fallen out with my family and could no longer afford to entertain in my own home, I smoothed my hair and without fear or favour, stepped up to the bar and ordered an appetiser to wet my appetite, and in the same breath enquired about my whereabouts and the turned around signposts.

'Half a mile west of Banathorpe, and the signposts were turned by the Home Guards as a precaution to fox the Germans if they invaded our countryside!' The speaker withdrew from the shadow of the notice board carrying a tray of beer glasses polished to high heaven.

Having the inbred capability to distinguish sounds and faces accurately, the brusque voice smarted like a cut and the well-defined features displayed a certain recalled severity which had then, and again now, set the tone that would not be easily grappled with. Woman-like, I didn't hold back on a smile – my beguiling smile – which I've been told, often, either set teeth on edge or sooths hostilities, but on this occasion I didn't care. It gave me time to collect my thoughts, after all, some curious instinct had led me here. 'Hello – again.' I sounded normal enough to my own ears. 'You're the first person I've spoken to today and the last person I expected to see here...'

'That's because you're an outsider and as I suspected from the brief encroachment the other day, you're out to revel and gather disturbing anecdotes from grown-ups who will almost immediately revert back to their bewildering childhood haunted by being unaccompanied and wearing labels tied round their necks with written identification too young to understand what the words evacuee and marshal yards meant!' All the wording was spoken through drawn back lips without taking a second breath, and the way he stated them made him a difficult opponent.

I held a pointed silence. Silences speak. Over the years of my childhood and adolescence, I chose to forget my own family. I believed they'd given me to Nanny, so I abandoned them. It wasn't selfishness. It was survival.

He drummed his fingers impatiently on the counter and stared blatantly back at me. 'You don't handle people like me!' The cobalt blue eyes when I looked directly into them revealed a commotion within their draw-well depths. I felt the hair follicles begin to rise, so to break the sensation I deliberately attended to my thirst, barely tasting the tang of the tomatoes as I regarded him over the rim of the glass, as another lesson of how not to catch a man in civil discord.

:

The early autumn sun had lost its heat and began to veil the scenery as I arrived at Banathorpe. First calling into the Post Office to enquire about favourable bed and breakfast accommodation. 'Mrs Maude Buelly,' I was told without hesitation. 'She runs a small-holding almost single handed, but she puts on a good plain meal – through her washing isn't quite white.' This was said in a no-nonsense way as I found myself being ushered to the door as though we were going to church, to quickly feeling the draft from the closing door.

:

Home Farm, I found quite easily on the outskirts of town.

Stone built, roofs slated, and sash windows with peeling paint which no doubt had seen better days. Parking my motor on the flagged forecourt, I alighted to view the immediate surroundings: poultry scratching about in the garth and garden, vegetables growing amongst flowerbeds, fruit bushes still bearing unpicked fruit and in the adjacent fields, mixed breeds of cattle grazed peacefully which evoked a sensation of euphoria to wash over me like a pervasion of flowers with fine thoughts. I felt as though I'd come home to stay.

Reluctantly, I turned my back on this tranquillity, and made a bee-line for the front door, knocking repeatedly before a dog barked, then hearing one, then two bolts slide backwards followed by a fob-chain, slung low, clattering to a stone floor – I reserved my inclination – was Mrs Buelly fit to be let loose? Then the door opened to reveal a lean woman with tousled silver hair, rosy cheeks, sapient grey eyes and wearing khaki overalls tucked into wellington boots.

'Mrs Buelly,' I said, giving a smile of intention. Recognising a woman who had to be cozened rather than given orders. In a flash of self-preservation I changed my name to Nanny's, 'I'm Eleanore Jarvis…'

'Yes, I know. The locals don't miss a trick. We heard that you'd called into the Gantlope Inn earlier and ordered a juice drink with Max, and I don't mind telling you he was a strange young lad, and I'd be surprised if you hadn't seen that for yourself…' She hesitated as if contemplating some unique destiny down a personal path.

I nodded, perhaps over-fast. 'He's not easy company by any stretch of the imagination…'

'Better alone than in the wrong company, and I can vouch for that.' Her voice sounded gruff but diffident, perhaps a trifle wistful. 'I believe that his young mind had been high-jacked. He use to sit on my garden wall every Saturday tea-time, in all weathers wearing his gas mask.' Mrs Buelly pushed the door wide open and stepped outside to pinch petals off polypetalous flowers planted in a stone trough beside the front door step. 'Max and five other evacuees stayed with the Pearsons, who ran the Gantlope Inn throughout the war years and later on. It was rumoured the boys worked all hours cleaning the pub from top to bottom every day to addle their keep. No wonder they looked like lost souls – then he left – and that's when I missed him. And I cried.'

It's hard not to warm to Mrs Buelly. The farmhouse is almost too full of furniture; sofas and easy chairs faded, with seating impressions, and the flagged stone floors covered at random with hand-clipped rugs tripping everyone up – especially the two other guests who came and went hastily after being scolded by our hostess for eating their own food secretly in the conservatory. 'Bloody cheek,' she snapped as we waited for the tea to brew, raising an eyebrow at me, then consolingly pushed a pottery dish of assorted nuts onto the kitchen table. 'I'll walk you round our rural town just to familiarise you with places of interest in case you're asked.' She crunched on an almond nut. 'I use to be the school secretary, so I was naturally asked to draw up a list of local children including evacuees from the registration book, particularly the ones who attended during 1939 to 1945...' She paused chewing, and looked at me in an intractable way, 'and I don't remember your face or your name, I mean, who would forget a ginger haired pupil with green eyes?'

I made a gesture of defiance. 'Well, it's rather a long story...'

Relaxation was not the message to put across faced with Mrs Buelly's explicit manner. Playing for time, I flashed my exquisite, troubled smile which Nanny use to say: 'Makes your plain face and freckles look brilliant.'

Mrs Buelly slowly closed her eyes on me and appeared to give herself over to intense thought, then just as slowly she opened them wide. 'Just for a moment there, Eleanore, you reminded me of someone I use to know... Someone who treated me like a malleable portion of his past.'

I gave a little uncomfortable laugh. 'Someone you knew in the war years?' I needed to know otherwise, how was I to know? Who?

She stared back at me. Had her eyes gone ice-silver? 'Yes and no! He always liked to present himself as a true gentleman... old money protected him and his lack of shame.

He had it coming to him!'

:

I slept sound enough, but woke with no real satisfaction. Why had I woken up so early? My brain scanned for seconds – then found that cold space of loss that I've carried inside myself from young memory – to a spark ignited by Mrs Buelly's impromptu remark. I closed my eyes to veil over her momentary comparison – that would be expecting too much – and where did Mrs Buelly stand in the matter? Had she a convenient selective memory or had she few reticence when it came to affairs of the heart? As Nanny use to say: 'The skill lies in objective interpretation.'

The house was quiet. No sign of Mrs Buelly's whereabouts. So I wandered outside. The morning was still and hazy. In the distance I could see corn stubble fields of cadmium yellow, and the trees, darkly green in contrast, signifying the oncoming of shedding their leaves – a cold reminder of the family estate before the legal seizure by the bailiffs. They came. We went!

Father, the obscure Peer, always the absent one, wasn't missed, but now Nanny was. The last time I visited her she was so pleased to see me I thought she'd never stop wringing her hands together. 'My darling, James...' Her laughter was as animated as a child. I was shocked! Nanny had mistaken me for Father... and simultaneously she rose from the chair. She thought he'd come to take her back to Wrothwaite

Estate, and out of the residential home. Then just as suddenly, Nanny sat down and her eyes rolled back into their sockets, then her face went blank. Totally blank. She had gone somewhere, some other place. Nanny no longer knew me. I'd turned and fled. And standing on the forecourt of Home Farm, feeling slightly unhinged, my face pouched by stress, I blurted out shamelessly, 'I hated seeing the back of someone I loved.'

'I heard that woe begotten eulogy, Eleanore. You sound as though you need a friend or at least an acquaintance, and it's more common than anyone would think.'

So consumed with my own grief, I had been unaware of Mrs Buelly's attendance at my elbow. I mumbled an apology saying something like, 'I've had so much good behaviour visited upon me that I'm always carelessly pleasant, and –'

She cut me short. 'I feel at a loose end myself. I've finished sweeping down and mucking out the cow-houses, so let's go inside the house, and I'll start making our breakfast.' She swilled her wellington boots under the yard water tap, then smiled benignly. 'Farm work isn't a job for anyone with a glass back, and it doesn't allow for elegant conversation. My cooking often shows my resentment.'

'Then I'll cook breakfast for us, besides, it will give me a chance to pump you for information about –'

Mrs Buelly raised an eyebrow. 'The way you said that, Eleanore, I can tell you've commonised your accent, so you can tell me what's brought you to Banathorpe.'

:

The morning mist had lifted and the sun shone warmly down on us from a pale blue sky. Dressed in pre-war dresses, fairisle cardigans and court shoes we sauntered along the outskirt road leading directly into town, talking, smiling, talking while missing out the finer details, '…and what about you, Eleanore?' Mrs Buelly was saying – again – 'and why Banathorpe?'

The suddenness of the dual question caught me off guard. My feet became somewhat ill-disciplined as I lurched from the grass verge to gravel. 'Why not Banathorpe? I'm a team member of the Redemption Bureau, a confidential out-house. The brand speaks for itself.' I felt a stab of nerve pains in my solar plexus. 'And as you ask so concisely, I can only say that I'm following up information leading to a missing war orator –'

'Lord Wrothwaite!' said Mrs Buelly, just as though she'd been asked. 'I knew there was something familiar about you, Eleanore. It's the way your feet turn inward when you walk… and the freckles…' She gave me a disarming smile – bold to excess. Shameless. 'I'm reminded of how I use to count them all on his body while he was asleep.'

Not easily undone, but on occasion, violent, I had to restrain myself, seeing the tears behind her eyes. No one ever saw my tears brim. I was always sent to my room to spill them over. Nanny saw to that! It's a dangerous business the shaming of the self.

We fell into step again, she broke the silence. 'During the war years I served as a locum secretary for the local Independent Party. James use to hold a monthly surgery in the municipal room for his constituents who had any problems and there were many – women – they fell scandalously in love with him – and yes…' She nodded her head in a flagellant way, '...we had an affair – briefly – he was as common as a cold, had no idea what an obnoxious effect his boastful, superior attitude could have on others, particularly his lady friends exposed to shame as much as to his waggery loving. When asked do you love me, James? He simply buggered off!' Her tone sounded droll, but carried entangled implications. 'Women can be as playful as men. We just do it differently.'

I didn't feel disposed to argue, so I held my silence on hearing the distant sounds of the local brass band playing wartime medleys. The familiar tunes lifted our spirits no end.

'We use to fox-trot to that,' Mrs Buelly's face lit up. A smile settled on her mouth and when an exuberant uump-pah-pah uump-pah-paa spontaneously blended into another melody, she laughed. Her eyes sparkled. 'Everyone use to hokey-cokey to this.' And she began to sing – 'You put your right foot in, and your right foot out... and you shake it all about.' And linking her arm through mine, '…come on, lass.

Let yourself go,' as she sang, 'in-out, in-out and shake it all about, that's what it's all about. Ooh-lay!'

Mrs Buelly is contagious. Just like a virus. I must not be smitten, or I may not want to leave.

Entering the field where the exhibition and demonstration stalls were erected, all adorned with wartime slogans which I'd read about, but having had a sheltered upbringing ensconced between Nanny and housekeeper, I'd become fatter and education became thinner…

Mrs Buelly broke into my thoughts with casual persuasion, 'During the war years it was considered important to have the right mental attitude to feeding the family, of course, popularised by the ration books.' She paused because I knew she wanted me to listen and notice other interested bystanders in front of the Women's Institute stalls demonstrating.

'Back to Basics. Austerity Fare…' A voice could be clearly overheard saying, 'Potatoes not rationed, but flour was, so to compensate for the shortage we used half cold mashed potatoes to half flour to make potato bread, pastry, cakes, scones, pancakes. Marzipan to mock fillings…' And as she continued to talk about penny-pinching methods, samples were handed out to tasters, whose noisy exclamations filtered round and about us.

Mrs Buelly said, 'I can remember the first pancake I made with cold potato, flour and dry egg powder. It was like cardboard. My husband nailed it to the kitchen wall.' She suddenly looked calamitous. 'Strangely enough, he died taking part in reactionary tournament years later.'

'Did he overact or was he thrown by man or horse?'

'No! He was hit in the eye-socket by a javelin, died instantaneously. I wouldn't have grieved so much, but the Peer-come-Knight in armour, riding horse-back, couldn't hit the bull's eye on a dart board.' She came out with it quietly, and damningly in her pleasant voice.

It was enlightening information in view of the circumstances. Too near the knuckle – I shuddered. 'Tell me later.' But later the moment had passed, as every now and then, Mrs Buelly met someone she knew, so briefly paused or somewhat longer as they reminisced in friendly terms. I was introduced as her bonhomie friend from over yonder?

'Call me Maude for heaven's sake,' she said amiably, as we moved on passed the asterisked dishes being demonstrated and tasted. 'Carrots!' She sighed. 'Cut into shapes then cooked to deceive the eye into believing them to be peaches or apricots, and Jerusalem artichokes made into scalloped dishes that suggested fish in appearance and even cut-out giving the optical illusion of oysters, and over there...' She pointed at the mock Ministry of Food stall with reproduced posters urging people not to waste food. 'Food is Ammunition of Wartime.' Maude looked scornful. 'Most of us lived from hand to mouth. Suet pudding on a daily basis with tiny scraps of corn beef and herbs, cut cold for teatime…'

Without a minimum of careful thought I said, 'Nanny use to say our consolation was having the country estate because farmers were exempt from wartime services, and the government dictated and subsidised what had to be grown to meet the needs of our country, subsequently, the surplus found its way into the black market business and…' I stopped my outpour of words on seeing Maude's unexpected tilt of her head making her silver curls bob around her rosy face, giving an indication to varying resentment. And all at once, I felt I'd been lured into false security, so before I could panic, I fell back onto bringing Nanny back to life. 'Nanny said it was Father's cavalier behaviour and his excessive braggadocio that polished him off.'

A slight uncomfortable silence came between us, wherein I felt plump against her leanness. I began to perspire, conscious of the heat emitting from the calor-gas cookers and the rising crescendo from the band players. It all became too much for me. I touched Maude's arm. 'Shall we head for the tea-tent? I'm feeling a little queasy… the gas fumes…' I'm not sure she said what I wanted to hear.

:

Max didn't walk, he strolled near the entrance of the refreshment tent. He was selling raffle tickets, and as we approached, Maude brightened noticeably. 'I've always had a soft spot for Max. He came back here after twenty years and bought the Gantlope Inn when the Pearsons retired. How he became self-made, I've never asked him, and he's never offered details so the curiosity vanished. The rumour was the Pearsons had invented him, so that was that.' As the distance between us closed she cooed to him. 'Grand to see you, Max, and I do believe you've already met my new friend, Eleanore Jarvis.'

'Yeah!' He looked obscurely at me as though she was trying to foist a damp baby upon him.

Max was obviously falsifying his own excellent imagination. I needed to disrupt his temperance – so I smiled demurely, remembering Nanny's rebuke – 'Don't show all of your teeth at once, Isabella, or you'll look like a mare looking over a five barred gate.'

So I veiled my beautiful green eyes with my sandy eyelashes reducing him to a shadow. 'My impressions of you Max, is that you speak to women as though we are inferior.' I turned to Maude and attempted a smile of sorts, 'and I wouldn't be at all surprised if he was raffling a piebald ferret or a left handed cricket bat.'

Maude laughed. Bless her.

Max placed himself in front of me. 'And you're not Eleanore Jarvis, because I remember seeing her at the Gantlope in 1944, where I and other evacuees were billeted throughout the war years.'

Stricken by curiosity, I blurred out, 'Nanny – here – at the Gantlope Inn!' We circled each other with an amorous enmity that called for constant wariness, myself sensing something was about to happen.

'You pronounced Nanny in a spirit of selfishness and the privileged.' His lips moved to form that dangerous smile that wasn't a smile, 'and you're certainly not local, so who are you? And what brings the likes of you to our neck of the woods?'

Sharing a mood as two rarely do with such stealth, the unobtainable becomes available. 'You're quite right. I'm not local. My name is Isabella and I work at the Redemption Bureau out of town. I'm here on behalf of a family concern… a missing person by the name of Lord Wrothwaite who represented the parliamentary constituency here in Banathorpe before and during the Second World War.'

He didn't answer me. Instead he turned to Maude who was busy swotting midgets congregating round her silver hair. 'You'll be coming later to the Gantlope. We've a Home and Away darts match and Lord Wroth Wroth's Lovies' Society are plating salmagundi sandwiches between potato bread followed by the Barn Dance.'

'We'll be there. It will be lovely to see the girls again. They'll be young, but no longer young, and nostalgia will take the edge off reality.'

'Lord Wroth Wroth's Lovies,' I repeated feistily, telling

myself that I must not trail behind as the lapwing trails her wings. I settled my brilliant smile upon her. 'Would you kindly introduce me to the Lovies tonight, Maude, or are you going to tell me the connection must not be questioned?'

Maude responded with affability. 'Don't you know, El… Isabella, women who understand men are unreliable allies, besides…' She paused to take her shoes off. 'If the ruling was despotic it was also imaginative with a sense of the ridiculous, and by consequence things got rather out of hand.' She sighed deeply and began to walk bare-foot across the grass with her shoes in her hands. 'Hurry up,' she called over her shoulder, 'I'm going to order a pot of tea and I don't want it to stew.'

On my suggestion – so I could keep Max in my eye-view as he strolled, conversing, on the periphery – Maude and I sat outside on the municipal bench taking our tea and a potato and flour scone. Her convivial voice broke into my chasing thoughts. 'How would you describe the Austerity Fare bake, 'Bella?'

'Eeh… uummm… I'm impressed. It's so moist.'

Maude looked at me quite strangely. I felt myself curdle. She reminded me of Nanny.

'That remark – moist – rings a bell!' She lowered her eyes to stir her tea thoroughly. 'Listen to me and don't say one word until I finish speaking, because I'm going to tell you something secret and you'd better keep it under your hat otherwise you could fall into the same trap.'

'Yes.' I couldn't say less.

'Your father, Lord Wrothwaite, was invited as a guest speaker at the Gantlope Inn's Home Front Fare in 1944. He was nauseatingly enthusiastic when he took to the rostrum, thanking the Women's Institute members for their outstanding simplicity, saying how pleasant it was to see the British people adherent to the old ways where plainness was signified and scarcity was being embraced with such stoicism – then, so James-like he waved aloft the presented potato bread loaf, shouting obnoxiously how he was simply astonished by the moist quality of potato bread, and as he had no immediate family he would be sharing it with his ministry colleagues!' Maude reflected for a moment. 'It was Nanny Jarvis whose shark-like instincts spotted him throwing the loaf into a dustbin. With bullish determination, she rounded up his ex-lovers – and there were many who'd heard his patronising oratory, and acknowledged, His Lordship had a misogynistic and masculine side to him which needed to be addressed at once...'

I held my breath – she was taking her time getting to the point.

'There's an old customary gantlet punishment, whereby the culprit, Lord Wrothwaite, was compelled to run down the outside passageway at the Gantlope Inn between two ranks – updated of course – by two rows of his ex-lovers to receive descending blows from each woman's rolling pin!'

'Gracious me.' I didn't know whether to laugh or cry.

'Nanny Jarvis had the foresight to remove his false dentures. He was carried off. Dead. Cremated.'

We sat in wordless companionship sipping our tea, while looking at the crowds drifting away, until Maude broke the silence that speaks. 'Burt will have brought the dairy cows from the fields and into the mistals for their second milking of the day, and the calves need feeding again, today.' She smiled into my face. 'See you later, 'Bella Somebody.'

Knowing I had not to be left behind, I walked towards Max feeling inside, deep inside myself, there was a certainty that something was going to happen. It could be next week, next month, next year, but something was going to happen; and I would be ready!

SPAGHETTI HAT

"A sophisticated lady who knows the worth of simplicity, wherein, connections between her alibi must not be examined..."

:

SPAGHETTI HAT

:

Jean Summersgill is a very busy lady. Her neighbours would go as far as to say, 'She just makes work for herself'. Others, more polite than their contemporaries, would murmur, 'That's what you do when you live on your own'. But Jean Summersgill is not disturbed about herself. She is her own woman. If acquaintances are about to impinge on her scheduled diary by inopportune knocking on number 37's prismatic front door, the lady of the house has a very reliable alibi. A coat-stand, whereupon, a selection of seasonal hats are at hand. When a polite tap-tap develops into attention seeking knocking, but still not quite abrasive enough, they feel to be heard within, thereby, giving Jean Summersgill a chosen moment to select an appropriate hat to wear for when she opens the door to pedestrian callers.

If the caller is someone she knows and likes, or somebody who will fill a gap with a friendly yarn, she'll smile invitingly and say, 'Hello. How lovely to see you. I've just come in.' However, if the visitor is someone she does not like or she's not in the mood to converse with, the opulent lady will say in a friendly, but not too friendly voice. 'Sorry. I'm just going out.'

These catch-words are used without self-consciousness. Jean Summersgill is a sophisticated lady who knows the worth of duplicity.

Until today. For some reason, a reason she could not even begin to remember. All she could recall was that she did not feel too good. She really did not.

The uncalled for moment happened while talking to herself in third person, a jug of hot coffee in one hand and a glass of fizzing bicarbonate-of-soda in the other, when she heard a familiar rat-a-tat-tat on her front door, and for once, Jean's home-guard strategy went clean out of her head.

'Hello!' she called in a discordant voice. 'Do come in.' Barely had she time to alter her suffering expression, when the door burst open, and there, framed in the doorway, stood, Muriel!

Caught on the wrong foot, Jean acquiesced, scarcely able to think past her throbbing headache. 'Mu… ri… el?' she said almost rendered speechless. 'Muriel!'

'Dear Jean. Hello. It's lovely to see you, again.'

They stared back at each other. Jean seeing a stouter person than she remembered, now shabbily dressed, no longer young, with an apologetic expression of one who needs a friend or at least an accommodating acquaintance, and as her eyes swept downwards her headache suddenly took a stab for the worst, giving her more than enough to think about – the additional presence in the form of luggage, sufficient for Jean to know by trial and error that the caller intended to stay, and the need to sit down became almost over-powering.

As for Muriel, she could see clearly, Roland's first wife had hardly changed at all in the last fifteen years. Her beautiful porcelain-like face ordinarily portrayed nothing, but today, superimposed one expression after another – as Roland use to say – 'Dear Jean is a stranger to common anxiety, never once been short of money or impeded by poor-health or the state of her own soul.'

'How long do you intend to stay?' Jean managed to convey by her tone that such short notice was unreasonable and most inconvenient to her active lifestyle.

'As long as you'll have me. I've got nowhere else to go since I lost Roland… then the house.' A smile came and went, and her eyes waited on the other for a favourable answer.

'Why me?' Jean kept a grip of herself. She knew Muriel's hopeful look. 'It's not as if we're on speaking terms, the last Christmas card you sent me, you wrote a scanty paragraph the size of a label pasted to a pot of homemade jam.'

Muriel had the grace to blush. 'If nothing else, if not nothing else, at least being here with you means there's someone I can trust who will hear me when I scream.'

Jean's smile scalded her. 'Have you not considered for one moment that it's rare for two ex-wives to fit comfortably under the same roof, not to mention fitting under the same man?'

'But we did all that sharing when we were students...'
Muriel's disarming smile was her only defence.

'That was until Roland came to stay.' Jean closed her
harassed eyes in memory, as she tried not to follow through
in her mind's eye the breakdown of her marriage due to
Roland's whimsical, disturbing games, and Muriel's
reciprocating ways. Quickly she reopened them wide to
escape the past. 'The coffee is going cold. I'll be able to
spare you a few precious minutes before you leave...' She
looked at her watch. 'I have an appointment at one-thirty
which I must not be late for.' She flashed a distant spiritual
smile to give a touch of truth to the precautionary white-lie,
while leading the way to the sitting-room, where she hastily
began to pour out the coffee.

The other woman glanced fervently about to re-adjust
her senses to the room; a charming room in many ways. Still
looked rather like a sales room, with its faded purple velvet
sofa placed beneath the bay window, which she remembered
caught and absorbed the south-east sunlight and smelt sort of
peppery when warmly sat upon. And the same ornaments
were crowded together on polished surfaces, bookcases
displayed a wealth of knowledge, and pictures of taste hung
on the green emulsion walls. Muriel lowered her hungry gaze
to floor-level, noting the floral wool carpet Roland had laid –
still showing much evidence of hoover and footwear.

Suddenly, the urge to be mothered overwhelmed the uninvited guest. Careful to avoid the chairs that were hardly to be sat upon, Muriel sank down onto one of the more generous arm-chairs.

Regardful, seeing the needy child in her attitude, Jean acknowledged it only with her eyelids. 'About Roland,' she said abruptly, handing over a cup of coffee.

Muriel smiled bravely over the cup-rim. 'Roland has gone to the Canary Isles. He invested in a plantation of vines...'

'Just for the iron, I suppose.' Jean's mouth tightened. That clinched it. Roland's number two ex-wife intended to make a long stay of it. She placed her fingers to her throbbing temples... had she said twelve-thirty or eleven-thirty?

Never one to let a thought go unsaid, Muriel looked quizzical at her old friend. 'You did say one-thirty, or perhaps two-thirty?'

A flush suddenly came to Jean's pale complexion. Rising too quickly to her feet she had to steady herself against the writing desk to let the wooziness spin itself out of her head.

'Do you remember our spaghetti time?'
'No!'

'Of course you must.' Muriel poured herself another cup of coffee. 'The reward of late night studies. All the gang looked forward to our keeping the faith in Friday night spaghetti-time, and I've decided that I can't live on the streets keeping myself half-dead, and my solution seems to be to live here with you.' She sank back onto the chair. 'From now on, I've decided, I'm only going to be influenced by the happy moments of my past.'

'All I need is peace and quiet, so would you please go away. It's kind of you to call, but please just go, now!'

'I only want a niche here just to tide me over until I manage to think well of everyone else…'

'The last time you moved out, I was left in the house, as was the dust and egg on the spoons.' Jean pointed a foot in the direction of the door. 'I'm going upstairs to freshen up for my meeting, and, when I come downstairs, I will expect you to be gone and what's more, taken your luggage with you.'

Muriel's mouth drooped at the corners. 'Loneliness isn't just being short of people and single clubs are simply dull and antagonistic. From now on it's au revoir to hard chairs, repetitious questions, spasmodic church coughing and paranoid people…' She hesitated. 'I shouldn't be going on like this because it only feeds your prejudices.'

Jean refused to be buttonholed. 'Resilience doesn't desert women when their marriage is over.' She vacated the room abruptly and ascended the stairs with remarkable energy, when only minutes ago she considered herself ill.

She shut the bedroom door discouragingly behind her.

Soon, Jean descended the stairs. She paused to listen intently. Stillness. The other woman's unexpected arrival had unnerved her, and the luggage had said it all. Jean Summersgill didn't know whether to laugh or cry but she had no time to indulge in the extravagance of moods. Fleet of foot, the lady of the house opened the front door and closed it as oneness.

Settling herself onto the car seat, she headed for town. It was only as she parked the vehicle in the Arts and Craft allotted space that it dawned on her, she didn't have any appointments today. The lie had temporarily become the truth. Oh dear! Had Muriel seen through her white-lie? She knew what they both use to call a fib, in their student days – a softer expression of a lie – quickly she crossed herself, feeling a dire need for a recompense cup of tea.

Ten minutes later, Jean Summersgill sat alone sipping hot sweet tea while reflecting on Muriel, who, when she really came to think about her methodical habits that had very nearly drove her mad – switching lights off, leaving her at the writing desk sitting in a pool of light with darkness at its edges – no wonder she had not finished her debut novel – still unfinished – and all that hoovering disturbing her brilliant mind. Quite unconsciously, Jean began to speak aloud her imperfect thoughts which included the betrayal and encumbrances of Roland…

'Are you alright, dear?' the customer who had been an interested spectator, appealed to her from the next table. 'You sound quite confused.' She reached out to the other's resisting arm. 'I think you're in need of a companion.'

Not able to trust herself to answer, Jean immediately vacated the chair. She needed solitude and the comfort of her own home.

Speedily she headed back to number 37, Wincroft Avenue, with disconsolate grating loudly on the changing of the gears, while unaware of gathering more speed and unprepared for the unforeseen roundabout, Jean braked hard, only to discover a sudden mechanical failure underfoot. Grabbing the handbrake for control, she swerved dangerously onto the outside lane of traffic to mercifully avoid a ten-ton lorry, yet unable to refrain from missing a transit van which slewed her vehicle precariously onto the circular island, where upon the car engine abruptly stalled.

Eight hours later, in which duration her car had been towed away, herself detained for questioning at the local Police Station, admitted and administered within the Accident and Emergency Department – released, then transported to number 37, via the Age Concern transit carrier. Traumatised! Jean Summersgill vacillated onto her doorstep, and what washed over her, she would never know, but she found herself channelled back to her carefree student days. Raising a resilient hand she rat-a-tatted quirkily upon the door the students' signature rhythm and thankfully, in response, hearing shuffling noises behind the door – followed by an unkindly long pause before the door opened wide, there stood Muriel, wearing their flamboyant, Friday night spaghetti-time hat!

They stared at each other. Muriel seeing the other's hair dishevelled around her proud porcelain-like face, revealing discolour surrounding a nasty swelling, and furthermore a white sling supporting her right arm with protruding bandaged fingers.

'Dear Jean,' Muriel shuddered in sympathy. 'I can see you won't be finishing your debut novel this side of Christmas.'

Jean's eyelids quivered sublimely, then quite unexpectedly, she began crying – snorting – crying. 'You can stay here for as long as you like, or at least until you find your feet again.'

Muriel thanked her with her smile. 'But only as long as it suits me, or until someone with the strength and the means takes a shine to me.'

The smile was returned. 'Despite Roland, maybe because of Roland, who left me, and stole you away.' Jean Summersgill swallowed her pain, yet retained her smile. Just! 'Friendships, I now believe are a precious commodity in life and they can't be bought as easily as a sort after prescription.' She squared her shoulders bearing the blunt of her injuries without self-pity. 'After today, embarrassment will not anymore bother my moral impressions, I promise you, Muriel.'

'Dear Jean, you do look a sight for sore eyes, but it's still lovely to see you, again. Do come in.' She removed the party hat with her usual outgoing manner. 'As you can see, I've just come in.'

IMPROPRIETY

"A long suffering wife whose green-fingered husband receives an enlightening Christmas goodbye..."

:

IMPROPRIETY

(Monologue)

:

Sylvia, sixty-something, now living in circumstances which she calls, 'new opportunities'. She's sat at her mahogany writing desk reading a letter with a cup of tea at her elbow. She removes spectacles. Her face registers pleasantness.

It's always a real treat to receive a letter from Zelda, particularly in my circumstances, left in the family home – alone – after what seems like a lifetime of sacrificial oneness while at the same time merging my own identity into rearing the children.

She glances at the letter.

How are the children? Zelda writes. Children do make us worry. Here, I make no pretences. My children were quite conscience-stricken at leaving me alone with nothing to do. I listen to them, I think, amiably, and hold back the fact this was not what I had in mind. I have plans. After all, the children have left home. They don't need me, and I want my life back, besides, they are independent of anyone else, if they hadn't wanted a partner.

Pause.

Derek, my only son, quite dashing and dangerous, has already found himself a new partner. One who doesn't dress up in his mother's clothes. And Daisy, my other child, with her usual exquisite tastes, is getting married for the third time. Everyone knows however many times a woman re-marries, she'll always re-marry the same type of man. It's getting to be a bad habit with her, being an ex-wife on the payroll.

Pause.

Reading between the lines, Zelda eloquently keeps all condescension out of her letters, although she does skirt round my circumstances gracefully with a sharp nib, writing, that I should have shown more of my heart instead of indulging in low level conflicts. But in my own defence, and I'm no martyr, I found myself obliged to make certain contingency plans – lamentable but necessary. She's right of course, with hindsight. It wasn't in the forbearance but in the circumstances. But I'm not ready for tears or deprecating prayers.

Sylvia leans forward, holding her body perfectly still, as though listening or seeing a happening from a faraway room inside the house. Then she springs to life.

I sometimes, if I'm honest, talk to myself out of deference, otherwise I'll not be able to move forward, and without giving too much away, George, my silver haired husband of thirty-eight years, was quite obsessed by his lack of sexual loss, whereas I'd given up the notion of that nonsense years ago. To compensate I somehow managed to cajole him towards gardening, where he could indulge in the luxury of moods. The deal was that retirement wasn't supposed to turn into making perhaps into certainties – yet I didn't recognise signs and implications until it was too late.

Pause.

It was August Bank Holiday, if I remember rightly. I was preparing our afternoon meal of double portions of halibut and homemade hollandaise sauce, when on the spur of the moment I went down into the garden to pick raspberries to go with the digestible bavoroise – just a little extra I use to provide to keep George sweet, when I sighted George, again, taking that well-spoken naturalist woman from the horticultural college on a conducted tour of the garden, his idyllic garden, whereupon I witnessed impropriety taking place behind a rhododendron evergreen. She wasn't the first. She was the first woman he could not, would not give up.

Sylvia puts a hand over her mouth, then slowly lets it fall onto her lap.

I'll never forget that night as long as I live. It was Christmas Eve, and I'd just finished sweeping up the fallen needles from the Christmas tree when George spoke in a cool, dry voice. His eyes rested a moment on mine, then he turned his back on me. 'Don't bother setting a table-place for me on Christmas day,' he said, 'because I'm leaving you to live with Rossvetta, my soul-mate, in her charming house on the outskirts of town.'

Pause.

It took a few moments for the full meaning of his words to penetrate my mind, meanwhile it wasn't as though I'd planned to give my hands something else to do besides wringing them, other than to recall how often I'd stared at the back of the silver splitter's head and recalled how he'd laid with his back to me, and how often I'd wondered how best to kill him. In consequence of that, without preparation, perhaps became a certainty. I simply moved back to the Christmas tree already decorated with a multitude of fairy lights and instantaneously switched them on, just before gardener George, silver splitter George in search of greater thrills, poured a kettle full of water over the dried-out coniferous tree roots.

Lights fade into darkness.

DAGGERS DRAWN

"A Women's Institute secretary takes perverse pleasure in usurping an old rival – the reinstated chairwoman, and finds herself much read about in a most unsuspected way..."

DAGGERS DRAWN

I wouldn't call myself a keen gardener, and neither would Yvonne Curlew, the chair-person of the In Bloom committee. It's common knowledge that I've never been one of Yvonne's clique, simply because our local paper had printed my miss-spelling of her name – Evone Cowyew. Well, years ago, she did cut off one of my golden plaits, and confidentially – Women Institute reporters are hardly Yvonne's forte. She probably thinks we're still using newspapers between our bed sheets, and still making carpet slippers and bags out of flat caps as we did during the rationing years of the Second World War.

I would be the first to admit that it was mere conjecture when I was voted in as secretary of the In Bloom committee. There was nothing peculiar about the motion made by Connie Lambert, a farmer's wife from the Upper-Dales, sat obscurely on the far aisle, who randomly nominated me, and an unforeseen outsider volunteered to second the proposal… much to my surprise and Yvonne's indignation.

From what I gathered, that night, Yvonne Curlew is a stickler for the Latin terminology… quick off the mark to rebuke incorrect pronunciation. In my own defence, and I'm no Judge, I was never taught to grasp the nettle of Latin idiom. Yvonne Curlew may be a good woman, once you get to know her, just misunderstood. I had the same problem with the Laughing Cavalier.

Keeping an ear to the ground… the reinstatement of the chair-person was not entirely unexpected, after all, Yvonne is not a loner. She's always inviting amusing and controversial people to share her house-parties, and it stands to reason that one or two locals are bound to talk out of turn; let things slip. Four years ago she had presided over our village, Middlesthwaite, entering the Town & Country In Bloom Summer Awards, when we won the silver gilt trophy which awoke public awareness and consequently, gained coverage in the Ramblers' Diary pages.

It's odd when one comes to think about it, how easily things come back to me. How every single, small remembered fact, seems instantly to remind me of another… in fact… if I had to be strictly truthful, I would have to say, I could write a book purely centred around the In Bloom society members, and acquaintances, especially Yvonne Curlew's eccentric house-parties. Naturally, I'm sworn to secrecy, but I can disclose, for now, our chair-person is a connoisseur who knows the value of artlessness.

Finding I had rather a large gap to fill in my diary, I arrived early for the first, In Bloom committee meeting, held in the town library. She, Yvonne Curlew, was already seated at the head of the top-table, on her old chair, wearing a gaudy dress, not new, and the colours were, I noticed, inclined to drain her complexion and emphasised her determinedly blonde hair.

Yvonne didn't blink an eyelid as I advanced towards her. I managed a smile. It was not returned. Not easily put-off, I approached the sacred top-table while seeing the whole surface was covered by photographs from her previous In Bloom competitors. Some snaps portrayed contestants clutching shields for all their worth, others trying to look pleased but their mouths gave them away. I behaved, I think, with discretion as I manoeuvred a few pictures aside to almost position my carpet bag on the polished space while making moves to sit alongside her. She elbowed me away with habitual railway signal gestures.

'Delorus Douvall,' she addressed me by my pseudonym. 'I don't want you to be a desk wallow. I need you to be sat out front with the rest of the committee members…'

To cover my irritation, I said, 'Like a row of turkeys looking forward to Christmas.'

Yvonne raised a pencilled eyebrow. 'I can see you'd be a real party-pooper with your exacting curmudgeon ways. No wonder you cling to the Women's Institute like a child does to its mother's ever ready hand.'

I forced a smile. 'It's only by practising the strictest discipline on myself, Yvonne Curlew, that I can manage to write well of everyone else which includes you.'

Yvonne sparkled. 'I owe it to myself and my conscience

to take risks and get results, besides...' She rearranged the snap-shots. 'I like to see people's faces at eye-level.'

With deliberation, I slowly sat down opposite her whereby our eyes reflecting only the face that looked into them... she acknowledged me with her familiar stare.

Breaking the tension, the next committee member to arrive was Connie, who, after the electoral meeting, confessed why she had voted for me on the spur of the moment... apparently she had been feeling fatigued because she and her husband Fred, hadn't been to bed for three weeks due to the lambing season, and seeing me stood next to the coke stove, pen and paper in-hand, reminded her of a cousin somewhere, who hadn't kept in touch. I did notice at the time, (I'm good at observation) how her mouth drooped momentary, then quickly curved upwards. Connie's like that. Friendly, but not to the extreme.

No sooner had Connie set foot through the doorway, she began to complain about the library flight of ascent and as she headed for the top-table, still talking – saying, she'd come to a stop every few steps to catch her breath and let the sensation of nausea settle down. The chair-person sprang from behind the top-table. 'Connie, dear, I don't want you to paint yourself into a corner.' She took a dexterous grip of the other's resisting arm and jostled her onto a front row seat, and as a consequence, Connie, still out of breath, rummaged through her handbag for an inhaler.

'The worst of it is...' She gasped, between drawing in and expelling out. 'The male element of...' Dear Connie, involuntary coughed away the rest of her words. Words lost in uncomplimentary noises.

'Pollen!' I offered, shuddering in sympathy. Then I moved next to her, to strike her gently on the back.

Around this time, Ray Biggerdyke, grocer, arrived carrying a self-advertising bag full of cuttings, stating that his flowers never looked anything like the pictures in the seed catalogues. He picked up a chair and headed towards the top-table.

Yvonne Curlew met him halfway. 'I didn't catch your name.'

His smile was encouraging. 'When you last knew me, Yvonne, I was Lear, in the Tempest. We performed in your Orangery. Remember?'

'No!'

'But I do.' Connie had now regained her countenance and I detected a hint of roguishness crept into her voice.

I wrote a memorandum... while Ray was unwillingly diverted to the front seats.

Next to arrive was Jessie. A contemporary artist and keen gardener. She's won no end of prizes with her chrysanthemums at local exhibitions. I've been in and out of her greenhouse for years, but never her home. She came hatless and bag-less. 'Sorry I'm late,' she said, 'but I was nabbed by someone on the doorstep.' She laughed. 'If he'd been dressed in pyjamas, I would probably have recognised him.'

Connie nudged me. 'There's more to Jessie than meets the eye.'

Jessie knows countless people. People from all walks of life. She's not shy, more an artisan. If she's not rattling a charity tin on a street corner, then she'll be spotted in the indoor market doorways busking, or selling raffle tickets to raise funds for the League of Friends, or you'll find her doing her twice weekly swimming strokes in the community recreation centre. She's all go, and very Jessie-like, she made a bee-line for the top-table, but I could see, Yvonne was more than ready for her.

'It's folk like you, Jessie Houseman who are so good at dealing with the science of gardening, which is more than I can say for your Latin…'

With more tinkling laughter, Jessie said, 'All that I can remember about him now, is that he had dark wavy hair with a trace of oil over it –'

'Like a well-tossed salad,' interrupted Connie, knowingly. She touched my elbow. 'I'll bet you anything, she was invited to Yvonne's house-party last weekend.'

'But Jessie's an octogenarian,' I whispered.

'So what! She's been assisting Yvonne for donkey years to stage-set a variety of shows in the Orangery.'

'You're pulling my leg…'

Connie handed me a lozenge. 'As far as I know, she still takes charge of the arrangements.' She crunched on the tablet. 'Helping them to dress and undress aesthetically while pro-offering artistic advice…' She coughed. Her eyes watered.

This managerial side to Jessie came as a complete surprise to me. So much so that my next memorandum completely wrote itself clean off the edge of my note-page. And before I had time to quiz Connie further, two other members suddenly appeared in the doorway like one's guilty conscience, bearing a tray, whereupon, infected stems and buds were placed for diagnosing later on in the meeting.

Caught off balance, the chair-person wavered between the pair of them, managing only to clutch hold of one member's hand and step boldly on the other's moving foot. Not wasting time on a greeting, she called across the room. 'Pests and diseases must be identified, unwelcomed though they are.'

This eulogy, I noted, produced a solemn atmosphere from the front row, even a slight aberration. The caretaker saved the day with importunity, by switching on all the lights in the room and instantaneously, we all screwed up our eyes against the sudden brilliance, to rapidly blink them open only to see blipped outlined images of the light bulbs.

Bedazzled. I retrieved my rapidograph pen from beneath

the top-table, while Connie kindly handed to me my dishevelled notepad. She spoke softly, 'You have a way with words. I hope they don't trip you up, my girl.'

Connie's eyes shone a little steely. But as I needed an aide to able and enable me, I decided to humour her. 'Not Latin.'

She half-smiled. 'A lot of concentrated work goes into shorthand. It's rather like Galanthus Nivalis. Very flirtatious!'

'You're surely not going to count my homely transgressions as sinful.'

She leaned closer. 'What did occur to me in one curious moment, you have the makings of a book in there... their Lupinus – your Lupins. Their Iberis – your Candituff.' She winked. 'Everyone lives a tale of a life transformed. If you find you have a few gaps to fill.'

'It's Friday today, how about Tuesday?'

'I'll probably go off the boil by then...'

'Perhaps Saturday or Sunday?' I tried to keep eagerness and even urgency out of my voice. 'Fish and chips on me.'

Connie frowned and fingered an ear-lobe. 'I'll not forego my Roast beef and Yorkshire pudding with dripping gravy for a fry-up, besides, I've got a party to go to this weekend. See you next Tuesday, Delorus Douvall.'

:

Tuesday, and it looked like rain. Undaunted, yet impatient, I stood, listening, with my hand on the front door handle, waiting to hear if Connie's option is for the back door. She can seem to be eccentric… I would hesitate to call it empathy because I'm not sure if a personality disorder can be said to have empathy. I'm still pondering on this matter when my guest passes the window on her way to the side door. Not prone to excitement, I rushed ahead down the passage, tripped over the hand-clipped rug which left no room for delay, before sliding the two blots backwards, then turning the key, just in time to compose myself and welcome her into my home.

'I hope you're offering plaice and not haddock,' she said, by way of greeting, which I thought lent a certain dignity to the occasion. It's all about heart.

I settled her down on the sofa, then handed over the fish and chips with mushy peas, and to give authenticity, still wrapped in last week's newspaper.

'You wouldn't catch Yvonne Curlew dishing out a meal like this…' And I couldn't help but notice, Connie didn't allow the full mouth of flat fish to prevent her from speaking. 'It's all bone china there and…'

'I live and eat very simple in my home, Connie Lambert,' I said, as I passed her the salt and vinegar glass wear while my eyes settle on her, willing her to fit into my expectations.

Taking her time, Connie looked expansively around my

living-room, then she splashed vinegar over her chips. 'Your home,' she said, 'is furnished in the style of the pauper. No wonder you want to better yourself through uninhibited writing. How far have you got with your novel?'

Not wanting to get to the point too quickly, I said, 'I'm in two minds Connie, whether to write my memoirs instead of –'

'What!' she stopped chewing. 'And who would want to read about the goings on behind the Women's Institute gatherings? That's the sort of dismal reading that calls for sleep and then impedes it.' She swallowed noisily. 'It would read like a ration book in the war years when we made do with ½ lb cold mashed potatoes to ½ lb of flour to make potato bread, and…' She paused reflectively.

Her words struck me as a little perfunctory, but they didn't disturb me. 'My job as a freelance reporter has, and is, a constant source of delight, Connie Lambert. I've diaries running for years which reveal an accumulation of –'

'Gossip! You don't want to fill your book with detritus! What you need are facts that you can embellish – glorify!'

My mind raced. This country woman's good nature was transparent, and her outspokenness was well known, and moreover indispensable to me. I needed her inside information to put some umbrage and oopsy-la-la between my story lines. A difficult problem to solve in an afternoon. 'How about a glass of port, Connie,' I said, feeling rather daring. 'Just for the nutriments.'

Connie raised an eyebrow perceptively, then wiped her mouth with her handkerchief. 'I hope it won't lay too heavy on the fatty meal. I have to be out of bed by five a.m. to help Fred hand-milk the dairy herd.'

After the second glass of port wine, Connie began to loosen up. 'Pleasure is a funny thing for colouring circumstances...' She giggled unexpectedly, then began to rock herself backwards and forwards and giggle some more.

Quite unlike me, I felt a sudden prang of jealously, being less pleasured myself, I was inclined to believe the feelings in my body were nurtured regrets or oncoming arthritis and...

'I did read some of your shorthand notes, Delorus...' She made tum-titummed tones. 'And I recognised the folks behind your fictitious names. Are you so sure you wouldn't want to be drummed out of the village?'

I acquiesced. It gave me time to think while replenishing our glasses. 'Don't be so sensitive, Connie. People seldom see themselves as others do, besides, I'm still at the plotting stage... I just need some nitty-gritty inside information to bulk out my story. Everyone knows I tend to be low-geared and phlegmatic. I'm not a bit like the furiously, witty Yvonne Curlew.' I saw a smile and threw one back without shame.

Smiling broadly, Connie waved aloft an empty glass. I hesitated momentarily. Was I passed the point of such fine distinctions? 'Please, help yourself, Connie.' And while she was acting on my invitation, I puffed up the flattened cushions and turned up the gas fire – a trifle.

Resting at ease, Connie threw caution to the wind. Names and events held within the Orangery began to fall like hailstones from a storm cloud, but I didn't seek shelter. My pen ran along page lines with the smoothness of cream down the back of a silver spoon.

After more than two hours, I gradually began to notice that Connie's voice kept trailing off. Words started to brush over one, then others. Shepherd, became th-eperd. Reasons changed to raisins – which caused laughter to drollery, not to mention ambience. I almost felt that I'd been there myself, then mercifully, Connie swooned clean away.

:

I've hardly had time to run a comb through my hair. The Delorus Douvall Diary was published by Haverdish and Eebygum last month and selling like hot cakes after being serialised in a national Sunday newspaper. Dear Connie can remember practically nothing about our Tuesday afternoon tete-a-tete, except, why – there she was policed and charged with over-the-limit while driving, causing a driver to swerve dangerously and hit a stone wall denting the other's car bonnet – all to be paid for – added to this, twelve months driving suspension. Naturally, Yvonne Curlew bailed her out!

As for the In Bloom competition our village won a bronze shield as recognition of the strong sense of community in the area; and low and behold my backyard patio with unrestrained geraniums, sweet-peas and rambling roses, twining with bind-weed (I don't believe in restraining – unlike Yvonne Curlew) won the individual plaque award. Apparently, my blooms had caught the indulgent eye of the Judge. He said, and here I quote: "It was as though the individual had captured a little corner of Latinity." Unquote.

:

The awards presentation was rather informal, held in the village hall, not the Orangery – as four years ago – the Mayor and Mayoress had earlier forwarded their apology for their cancellation, explaining briefly, that the Mayoral car was still awaiting a body spray due to a collision caused by a very reckless driver from the Upper-Dales.

She, Yvonne wore a remote smile – rather like the Mona Lisa – when she presented me with my Portella Award. In return I handed her a signed, Delorus Douvall Diary. Immediately, her manner suggested it was something indigestible. 'It won't wash with me, Annie What's-it! It's folk like you who entertain without having the expense of guests!'

With a show of geniality, I said, 'Just suppose that I interviewed you and asked you to describe yourself in a few words, Yvonne. What would you say?'

Her answer was no answer at all. The two words were not a description.

'I heard that,' said Connie, whose eyes were the only eyes I could catch as Yvonne turned her back on me. She patted the chair next to herself. 'I don't know about anything else, but I do understand the necessity to sit down.'

I thanked her with a smile and sat down, facing her. 'I'm so happy Connie,' I said, 'and I don't know how to express it… hardly dare in case it vanishes, and…'

'I'll be glad to see the backend of hay-time.' Connie scraped back her chair. 'I left Fred changing twisted tines on the tedder, and if he can't get them level, it's back to the rake and a two pronged hay-fork.'

I caught her arm. 'Before you leave, and you're the first person I've told, Connie…' I paused to take in deep breaths from happiness. 'It seems that I've obtained notoriety with my pen and ink. I've already been offered a commission to write a sequel to my Delorus Douvall Diary… and I'd love to write your life story, I really would.'

Suddenly Connie brightened under direct attention. She looked ten years younger. 'Next Tuesday.' She laughed. 'Fish and chips, on me.'

THE END

:

Thank you for reading SILVER SPLITTERS

Tales of the Unsuspected

:

_____A Proposal_____

:

Become a Tattle Head by following Gwen Hullah's author blog site – packed with:

Spot it – *Forth-write tips as told to Gwen by her fictional character Delorus Douvall...*
Script it – *Post your comments and pics all things Silver Splitters in-kind or out-kind.*
Scroll it – *Read Gwen's early extracts.*
Share it – *What draws you to tales of the unsuspected?*

To receive such truthisms in your inbox click <u>follow</u> at:

SilverSplitter.com

About the author

It use to be said, you could recognise a Yorkshire person by the way they don't suck, they crunch a boiled sweet! Gwen Hullah, (maiden name), was born and bred in the West Riding of Yorkshire. Educated at Braithwaite School, Dacre, and Pateley Bridge Secondary Modern, Nidderdale. By tradition in those days, farmers' daughters became home-land-girls wherein horse-power ruled – as the saying goes – 'Shake a bridle over a Yorkshire man's grave and he'll rise up and steal your horse'.

Married for twenty-eight years, Gwen resided in Grantham, Lincolnshire for most of those years. She became a free-lance writer, amidst other chance jobs – and the instigator of Radio Witham, Grantham Hospital Broadcasting Service in 1976.

Gwen has one daughter, Ida who is a musician singer/songwriter/guitarist (and author; pseudonym Zizzi Bonah) whom she's very proud of. They now live back home in Yorkshire.

'Wapentake' – revenge fiction – is a new writing genre created by Gwen to suit her style of writing. Her debut novel: Safe In Killer Hands – Money, Madness, Murder, is published by She And The Cat's Mother.